GIB
RIDES
HOME

ZILPHA KEATLEY SNYDER

A Yearling Book

Published by
Bantam Doubleday Dell Books for Young Readers
a division of
Random House, Inc.
1540 Broadway
New York, New York 10036

Visit us on the Web! www.randomhouse.com

Educators and librarians, for a variety of teaching tools, visit us at www.randomhouse.com/teachers

Fans can visit Zilpha Keatley Snyder at her Web site: www.microweb.com/lsnyder/

ISBN: 0-440-41257-9

Reprinted by arrangement with Delacorte Press

Printed in the United States of America

September 1999

10   9   8

OPM

To the memory of my father,
William Solon Keatley

CHAPTER

1

On a dark, cloudy afternoon in the fall of 1909, a strange thing happened on the third floor of the Lovell House Home for Orphaned and Abandoned Boys. Something so downright mysterious that even firsthand witnesses could scarcely believe their eyes. What those witnesses, five amazed and startled senior boys, saw that dull, gray afternoon was the sudden and entirely unexpected reappearance of a boy who had left the orphanage more than a year before.

No one had heard from Gibson Whittaker since he went away, but the rumor was that he had been adopted by a family who lived near Longford, a small cattle town in the next county. There was nothing especially uncommon about that. Half, or even full, orphans left Lovell House fairly often, going back with a remaining parent or out to an adoption, but what was so shocking was his reappearance. How could Gib Whittaker be strolling into the senior boys' dormitory when the law said, at least the law according to Miss Offenbacher, that Lovell House adoptions were not reversible? In other words, when you left the orphanage you left it for good and always.

The sun had already gone down when Gib arrived, and the third-floor Senior Hall was dimly lit. The supper bell was due to ring soon and the long hall, with its orderly rows of narrow beds, was almost deserted. Of the sixteen boys who were seniors that year, only five were in the room and they were running late. Since they'd spent their afternoon chore time mucking out stalls in the orphanage's barn and cowshed, more than the usual amount of changing and scrubbing had been necessary.

Being late for supper was dangerous, but so was arriving at the table in an unsanitary condition, so the situation was serious, but not quite serious enough to prevent a certain amount of fooling around. Some shoving and splashing was going on as the five boys crowded around the washbasin nearest the hall door. The water in the basin was cold, and gasps and giggles were echoing through the high-ceilinged room, when the shriek of door hinges caused a sudden silence. As one, the gigglers hushed, froze, and then turned anxiously, expecting Mr. Harding, maybe, or even Miss Offenbacher. But instead, there he was, Gibby Whittaker.

For a second, no more than a split second probably, nobody recognized him, not even Jacob Fetters and

Bobby Whitestone. And Jacob and Bobby had known Gib since back when they'd been little old juniors together.

But under the circumstances, Bobby and Jacob's blank stares weren't too surprising. After all, Gib had been ten years old when he went away and now he had to be almost twelve. He'd filled out a little, gotten some taller, and no longer had the typical Lovell House haircut—a near scalping by a local barber whose "orphans' special" was quick and cheap, if not particularly good to look at.

He was dressed differently, too. Instead of the scratchy wool suit of institutional navy blue, he was wearing a fringed leather jacket over mud-stained denim pants. And on his feet, instead of the standard orphanage clodhoppers, were a pair of boots. Scuffed and dusty boots, certainly, but with a style about them that had nothing to do with living in an orphanage, or for that matter anywhere else in downtown Harristown.

So the hair and clothes were different all right, but there were some things about Gib Whittaker that weren't ever likely to change. He was still lanky and tall for his age, with a slow and easy way about him, and a grin that did something to his eyes before it began to stretch first one side of his wide mouth and then the other.

So it was Gib sure enough, right back there in the third-floor dormitory where nobody had ever expected to see him again. But what made his reappearance even

3

more amazing was what he'd brought with him. What Gib Whittaker was toting into the seniors' dormitory, along with an ordinary old duffel bag, was what appeared to be an honest-to-God saddle. An honest-to-goodness old roping saddle.

"Gibby," somebody finally yelped, Jacob or Bobby probably. Gib grinned, and then, while the others stared like a bunch of dummies, he sauntered down the hall, dumped the bag and saddle on the floor beside bed number five, shoved them under with one foot, stuck his hands in his pockets, and nodded, first at straw-headed old Jacob and then at skinny-as-ever Bobby Whitestone.

"Jacob," he said, and then, "How you been, Bobby?"

A new boy, someone Gib had never seen before, was poking Jacob and whispering, "Who—who—who," like he'd been turned into some kind of big-eared, towheaded owl.

"Stop that, Jackie." Jacob elbowed the new kid out of his way. "Don't you know nothing? It's Gib. Gib Whittaker." But Jackie, who wasn't especially quick-witted, went on staring blank-eyed. It wasn't until Bobby Whitestone spoke up that Jackie and the other new boys began to understand. "You know," Bobby said, "the Gib we told you about, who got adopted a long time ago."

Jackie's "Ohh! That Gib," was long and drawn out as a sigh. They'd all heard about that Gib Whittaker.

Knobby-headed little Bobby Whitestone, who had been at Lovell House ever since Infant Room, was looking as walleyed as a wild mustang. Bobby had always been a worrier. And a whiner. His voice had a high-pitched wobble to it as he asked, "What happened, Gib? How come you're back?"

Bobby had good reason to be worried about Gib and about what might happen to him now. Everybody knew how dangerous it was to run out on an adoption. Especially to run out on certain kinds of adoptions.

Jacob Fetters, who, like Bobby, had been in Junior Hall with Gib, looked worried too, his blotchy face scrunched up into a twitchy grimace. "Where you been, Gib?" he asked. "Miss Mooney said you'd been sure enough adopted by some people near Longford. Some real rich folk, name of . . ." Jacob looked around, asking someone to help him remember. "Name of . . . ?"

It was Gib himself who answered. "Name of Thornton," he said solemnly. Then he grinned at Jacob and added, "The Thorntons live pretty near Longford all right, and I guess they're fair-to-middling rich. Miss Mooney got that part just about right."

Jacob nodded, and his sympathetic shrug said he could guess what Miss Mooney had been wrong about—the kind of adoption it was.

"Yes sir," Gib went on, his halfway grin hinting that there was something more to what he was saying than just the words, "I been with the banking Thornton family for almost—"

"Banking Thorntons?" Bobby asked.

Gib's lips twitched again. "That's right. That's what some people call them. The banking Thorntons. Own the only bank in Longford, matter of fact."

"But how come you're back, Gib?" Bobby's coyote whine had gone higher and wobblier, and his jittery eyes kept flicking from Gib's face to the saddle under the bed. "You didn't skip out, did you?"

Gib's eyes had a teasing squint to them as he answered. "You want to know if I just up and rustled myself a horse and saddle and ran off?" He looked around slowly, at Jacob and Bobby first, and then at each of the other boys, before he shook his head. "Naw," he said, "I didn't run off." His smile spilled over onto his mouth as he added, "And I didn't get here on horseback, either. Matter of fact, I came here in a motorcar."

They stared back, their eyes showing how amazed they were, and how relieved to hear that Gib hadn't done something so dangerous and foolhardy as to run away. At least Bobby and Jacob looked relieved. A couple of the other boys might have been—well, almost disappointed. The way they'd look, perhaps, if a public hanging they were planning to attend had just been called off.

Noticing how one of the new boys had started to ease off toward the dormer windows that faced Lovell Avenue, Gib's smile got wider. "What're you looking to see out there?" he asked. "A sheriff's posse, maybe?"

The new kid looked guilty, but you couldn't really blame him all that much. Wasn't any wonder he was expecting the sheriff or maybe something even worse.

Not after all the things Miss Offenbacher always said about what would happen to runaways.

"Well, what did happen?" Bobby was still whining. "How come you came back?" And then, as his eyes rounded again with a new and even more terrifying thought, "Offenbacher knows you're here, doesn't she?" he whispered, glancing over his shoulder. "You didn't just sneak in, did you, Gib?"

Gib was just opening his mouth to answer when suddenly the whole room was full of a harsh clanging noise. All five of Gib's observers jumped like scared jackrabbits, and then shrugged in embarrassment. Just that noisy old dinner bell, their sheepish smiles said, and with no further hesitation they all trooped out. Everyone but Jacob, who dashed back to give his face a last-minute splash before he rushed after the others, wiping his dripping chin on his shirtsleeves. Gib chuckled, remembering how Jacob always had to be extra careful because dirt showed up so much on his bleached-out skin.

Near the door Jacob paused long enough to ask warily, "You coming, Gib? You coming to supper?"

Gib shook his head. "Nope," he said. "Not tonight. Miss Offenbacher said she wants to talk to everybody first. Kind of explain things, I guess, before the old bad penny shows up again."

"But . . ." Jacob's pale face under its thatch of straw-colored hair was puckered with worry.

Gib went on, "It's all right. I'm not hungry. And anyways, I got something to eat there in my bag."

Jacob went out reluctantly, still looking over his shoulder. It wasn't until they'd all disappeared and their echoing footsteps on the old wooden stairs had faded away to nothing that Gib went back to bed number five. Number five had been Charlie Biggs, if he remembered right. Gib remembered Charlie. A funny-looking kid, with one off-track eye and spiky, no-color hair. Must be ten or eleven years old by now. Gib sighed, wondered about Charlie for a moment, and wished him luck before he sat down on the edge of the bed, pulled out his duffel bag, and took out Mrs. Perry's package.

The sandwiches were full of things no boy at Lovell House ever laid eyes on, lettuce and tomatoes and thick slabs of ham and cheese. They looked mighty good all right, but something was interfering with Gib's appetite. He ate a few bites, then rewrapped the package carefully and put it away. After he'd pulled off his boots, he flopped down on the bed with his arms behind his head, and began to try to face up to the fact that it was really true. He had come to live at the Lovell House orphanage, just as he had done once before—almost six years ago.

CHAPTER

2

When Gib tried to look back to the years before he'd come to live at Lovell House, there were only bits and pieces. He didn't know why. He knew he'd been about six years old when he showed up that first time, because Miss Mooney had told him so. But it surely did seem likely that in six whole years a person would store up a lot more memories than what he could call to mind. More than the few scenes that, even when they were bright and clear as life, seemed to be unconnected to any reasons or explanations. Nothing that told him what the memory meant, or what it had to do with where he'd come from, who he'd belonged to, or why he'd wound up at Lovell House.

Sometimes the bits and pieces came with a good warm feeling, but others had the look and feel of a bad dream. Like the sneaky one that usually came in the middle of the night, where he suddenly was watching a little boy riding in a buggy. A skinny-faced kid, with bony legs hanging out from too-short pants. He would be watching the kid in the buggy and then suddenly he, Gibson Whittaker, would be that little boy. Dressed in a dark blue suit with a big square collar he would be the one riding in a shiny new buggy behind a high-stepping dapple gray mare.

It was a good dream at first because someone, a big man in a scratchy wool coat, was letting him hold the reins and telling him how easy it was for good hands to talk to the gray mare. The big man didn't seem to be his father or even anyone he knew real well, but he had a kindly face, and knew how to make his hands tell the mare to step lively or slow down without using a whip or even a hard slap of the reins. And Gib was feeling happy because he could feel, plain as day, the talking between his own good hands and the gray's mouth.

But then the buggy was stopping in front of a huge building. A big old stone building that rose up like a mountain, with high gray walls that went on and on forever and, way down at the end, round towers that seemed to stretch up almost to the clouds. A castle, it surely was, like the one in the fairy-tale story about an evil king who killed everybody who opened secret doors or asked forbidden questions.

And then a woman in a big feathery hat was lifting him down from the buggy and he was holding back and trying to tell the woman about the castle and how he had seen it before in a book and how an evil king lived there.

10

He seemed to know the woman a little bit, but not enough to know her name except for Ma'am. "No Ma'am. No!" he kept saying. "Please don't take me there. Please don't."

Then Gib seemed to be just watching again, and the woman was pulling the little boy up a long, curving road toward the huge building. It seemed like a nightmare all right. The castle was way too big and grand to be anything like a regular house for living in. And even though it sometimes seemed he was just standing off and watching what was happening, Gib did have a notion that part of it might have been a true remembering of the day he'd come to live at Lovell House.

The rest of what happened that day had faded away, like everything and everybody who'd come before.

Even the memory of his mother, whose name had been Maggie—Maggie Ernestine Whittaker, according to Miss Mooney—was the same way, nothing but broken-off, senseless pieces. Nowadays all he could recollect for certain was the way her hair had wisped around her face on hot days, some parts from her songs and stories, and how her soft eyes went hard and sparkly when she got mad.

Remembering Mama's angry eyes always brought back one memory picture, sharp and whole as yesterday. The part that always seemed to come out the clearest was the old man and the horse.

Gib could recollect that old man plain as anything.

Could even see his long, dirty coat, and how it flapped around while he beat on a poor old horse with a two-by-four.

He could see that horse real clear, too, a skinny little swaybacked buckskin. He didn't know for sure just where the horse beating happened, but it might have been in a town because other people were in the picture, too. Maybe five or six men, who seemed to be just standing around watching the horse beater, and Mama and Gib in their buckboard. And then, all of a sudden, when the man was fixing to swing the two-by-four again, Mama kind of flew out of the buckboard and hollered right in his mean old face.

Gib could bring back the whole thing sharp as could be, most anytime he tried—the buckboard and the team Mama was driving, too, a big bay gelding and a sorrel mare. He was pretty sure the bay's name was Amos, but he wasn't sure about the mare's. He could remember how she looked, though, plain as anything. A dark sorrel she was, with a pretty blaze face and a spooky disposition. He seemed to recollect things like that real easy.

Sometimes he could even see how the old horse beater's straggly beard quivered when Mama yelled at him. And how he, Gibson, could only watch from the buckboard, because he was too little to get down by himself. Could only sit there crying while the old man stood glaring at Mama and holding the two-by-four up over her head. But finally the horse beater backed off and put his club back in his wagon. Gib could even remember how Mama's eyes had sparkled in a different way when some of the men who were watching waved their hats and cheered.

That seemed to be his clearest memory of all, which was a puzzling thing when you came right down to it. Why would a person remember his mother hollering at a dirty old stranger when he had so few other memories of those years before he came to Lovell House?

Oh, there were some other small scenes all right, ones he couldn't recall on purpose but that sneaked up on him now and then when he wasn't trying. Memories of hearing books read and songs sung at bedtime, and even parts of the stories and a few of the pictures in the storybooks.

And other times different bits and pieces came back, everyday things mostly, like gathering eggs, and feeding chickens, and other critters too. Lots of little bits of memory about feeding animals—particularly the horses.

Feeding the horses and riding them, too. At least riding gentle old Amos bareback, sometimes with just a hackamore on his long, bony head. Gib seemed to remember the riding, not just in his head but in other parts of his body, too. As if his legs and his backside could remember Amos's trot in the same way maybe that Miss Mooney's fingers remembered the keys on the piano. Another thing his backside seemed to recall was a spanking he'd gotten for trying to ride the other one—the spooky, hard-mouthed sorrel mare.

So there were things about animals, and stories from his mama's books, but nothing more about Maggie

Ernestine herself. Miss Mooney said that she'd died not long before Gib came to live at Lovell House, but he had no memory of her dying. And nothing at all about his father except his name in the record book. John Wilson Whittaker, deceased 1901.

And nothing about how he came to be in that shiny buggy on his way to become a Lovell House orphan.

CHAPTER

3

There weren't many places, no real towns or houses leastways, in Gib's early memories. Nothing at all that he could put a name to or find on a map. At least not before he came to live at Lovell House. And even his early orphanage memories were never clear and sharp, because all the early thoughts and feelings seemed to come tangled up with ones that came later. Memories, for instance, of crossing the entry hall on his way to the office.

The entry hall at Lovell House was very grand, with a slippery white stone floor and, on each side, staircases that curved up toward a faraway circle of darkly glowing colored glass. Sometimes it seemed to Gib that he could recall that shiny whitish floor below, and the soaring dome above, from that very first day when the woman in the big hat pulled him through the two sets of double doors and into the huge, dimly lit room. But maybe not.

Maybe he was only bringing to mind all the times he'd seen it since.

Memories of living in Junior Hall were tangled too. Any early recollections of his first few days as a junior blended into the days and months that came later. Being a junior meant that you slept in an enormous half acre of a room that had once been the Lovell family's private ballroom, with around thirty other four- to eight-year-olds. All the way from four-year-olds who cried in their sleep and wet their beds to eight-year-olds who took the bread you saved from supper and threatened to whup you real good if you told.

It seemed to Gib that all the best Junior Hall memories centered around Miss Mooney, who was freckle-faced and skinny and just about the busiest person at Lovell House. Besides being a classroom teacher and the housemother for Junior Hall, Miss Mooney was in charge of the house clinic, where she took care of things like smashed fingers and chicken pox. Gib had never minded being a little bit hurt or sick because it gave him a chance to talk to Miss Mooney without thirty other boys trying to horn in. It seemed to Gib that every time he got to talk to Miss Mooney she told him things that made him feel better in places he hadn't even known were hurting. Like when she told him about hope dreaming, for instance.

Gib was still pretty new at Lovell House the night Miss Mooney told him how to hope-dream. It was very late and most of the juniors had been asleep for a long time when she came into the hall. But Gib wasn't sleeping, and neither was a little four-year-old kid named Bertram. Bertie had been crying softly for a long time when Miss Mooney stopped at his bed and talked to him until he went to sleep. Then she came on down the hall and when she saw that Gib was still awake she stopped and asked him why.

Gib sat up. "I don't know, ma'am," he said. "I just can't get to sleep sometimes. Just thinking too much, I guess."

And then she told him about how to do hope dreams when you can't sleep. A hope dream, Miss Mooney said, was when you make up a long daydream story about something very good happening, the very best thing you could possibly imagine. And you picture all the places and people in the dream very carefully until you can see everything as clear as day. Then she started telling him about the hope dream she'd had when she was a little girl in Omaha, but before she'd finished, just like Bertie, he went off to sleep.

It was right after that Gib began his own hope dream about living in a family with a father and a mother and lots of kids and animals. His family always lived in the country, but as he got older Gib's dream pictures of the family and the house changed. At first the mother always looked a lot like Miss Mooney and the father was something like a friendly man Gib had seen once at the Harristown Library. As for the house itself, it started out rather small and vague, but whenever Gib got to go into Harristown, to the library or barbershop, he'd pick out houses to hope his would look like.

As the months went by, Gib learned how to get along as a six-, and then a seven-, and finally an eight-year-old junior. One thing he learned early on was that it was a good idea to steer clear of certain senior boys who liked to call juniors names like "runt" and "dumb little green-horn" and even twist their arms just to make them say uncle.

Sometimes Gib couldn't wait to be a senior even though some people said that juniors were the lucky ones. "Juniors get all the breaks," Gib remembered hearing, way back when he was only six or seven. Buster Gray had said it one day when he was in Junior Hall collecting dirty laundry.

"What breaks?" Gib had asked.

"What breaks?" Buster, a scrawny senior boy with a fuzzy upper lip and a crippled foot, looked amazed at Gib's ignorance. "Well, for one thing you get all the easy indoor chores in the winter time, 'stead of freezing to death shoveling snow or mucking out the cow barn. And you get to live down here in the big hall, 'stead of roastin' in summertime and freezin' to death in winter way up there on the third floor. Ol' furnace don't do much good way up there."

Gib nodded, thinking that Buster sure thought about

freezing to death a lot. And noticing, too, that Buster did look kind of frostbitten most of the time, particularly around the ears and nose. "Hadn't thought of that," Gib admitted.

"Yeah." Buster seemed pleased with Gib's response. But just as he looked to be winding up to tell Gib a lot more, Miss Mooney came in and Buster picked up his basket of bed-wetter sheets and hobbled on out.

As Gib went on with his own chore time that day, his own easy indoor chore, dusting the woodwork in Junior Hall, he thought about what he'd just heard. He could see what Buster meant, but at the same time it didn't seem to Gib that living in Junior Hall was all that easy, either.

Of course, all the teachers were always saying how lucky *all* the boys, infants and seniors as well as juniors, were to be living at Lovell House. And what a blessing it was that Mrs. Harriette Lovell, whose little son had died of a fever, had given her beautiful mansion to be used as a home for orphaned and abandoned boys. Gib guessed it was true, that he was lucky to live at Lovell House, but something inside him didn't seem to believe it.

The part that didn't seem lucky was not having a place and people to belong to. It seemed to Gib that not belonging anywhere or to anybody was just about as unlucky as you could get. And Jacob felt the same way.

Jacob, in fact, said he thought it was kind of funny how everybody wanted them to feel lucky. "Yeah," he said, "I felt specially lucky last Christmas when all I got was one orange slice and one little bitty peppermint stick. Didn't you?"

"Yeah, *lucky*," Gib agreed. Holding out both hands, pretending to be holding his slice of orange and piece of candy, he put a dumb grin on his face, and when Jacob did the same thing, everybody laughed. And that started the dumb lucky joke that he and Jacob kept fooling around with.

Once, even though he could pretty much guess what Bobby would say, Gib asked Bobby if he ever felt lucky.

"Lucky?" Bobby had said. "Me, lucky?"

Watching how his lips and eyebrows dipped down at the corners, Gib could just about tell what Bobby was going to say. Or at least just about how whiny it was going to be.

"You must be fooling. You must think being dumped outside a church in the middle of a twister storm is a real lucky way to start in living."

Gib had heard the story before, the one about the basket on the church steps and the twister that had just about carried Bobby away before the preacher came out and found him. But he'd also heard Miss Mooney's answer when Bobby asked her to tell Gib that it was true.

Miss Mooney was the only adult at Lovell House who would even try to answer questions like "Where did I live before I came here?" and "How come I'm an orphan?" Sometimes she even looked up your records in the head office, if you asked her real nice. After she'd looked up

20

Bobby's records she hadn't said that he was lying, but she hadn't exactly agreed with him, either.

Miss Mooney was smiling as she said, "It was a storm all right, Bobby. The minister who brought you to Lovell House said there was a rainstorm the night they found you." Noticing Bobby's disappointment, she hurried on. "A real bad rainstorm, I think, but I don't think there's anything about an actual tornado in the record book."

When Gib grinned and poked Bobby in the ribs he only shrugged, but the next time he told the story, the tornado was back again. Bobby was that kind of kid. The kind who seemed to enjoy thinking that something big and powerful had a grudge against him. A big enough grudge to stir up a whole tornado just to get a little newborn baby, and then, when that didn't work, to make him grow up to be a homely, knock-kneed, sickly orphan.

But, coyote whine and all, Bobby was mostly a good friend. At least when being friendly wasn't apt to get him into too much trouble. And Jacob was an even better friend. Jacob was the kind of friend who would stand up for you no matter what. No matter that Elmer Lewis had it in for you.

Elmer Lewis, a thin-headed, sharp-faced kid whose cot in Junior Hall was just three down from Gib's, was a natural-born tattler. Elmer would tattle on his best friend, and not just to get out of trouble, either. Elmer seemed to tattle just for the feel of it, like a chicken scratching even when there was nothing there to eat, just for the feel of the scratching. There was the time, for instance, when Elmer got Gib sent to the Repentance Room for something he didn't do at all.

It all started in Junior Hall one night when Elmer was scaring poor little Rabbit Olson to death, telling him how there was a ghost in Lovell House. Rabbit, whose real name was Georgie, had a long upper lip and a turned-up pinkish nose and was scared most of the time, even without any encouragement from the likes of Elmer. One night, when it was almost silence time and Georgie was already in bed, a kerosene lamp near his bed flickered and went out without a soul touching it.

"Hey, Rabbit," Elmer said, noticing how Georgie was staring at the lamp. "Did you see that? Must be that old ghost again."

"G-G-Ghost?" Rabbit said, ducking down so just his round rabbity eyes showed above his blankets, and right off starting to wheeze. Poor old Georgie always seemed to have a hard time getting his breath when he got extra tired or scared. "What g-g-ghost, Elmer?"

Elmer came back toward Georgie's bed, staring down first at him and then at the other boys who had begun to cluster around. "You hear that, men?" he said. "This dummy doesn't even know about our Lovell House man-eating ghost. What do you think? Maybe I ought to tell him."

"Yeah, you tell him, Elmer," someone said with a mean giggle.

"Suppose I should ought to," Elmer said. He sat down

on the edge of Georgie's cot and, while several other boys from nearby beds crowded around, started in on an awful story about a man in a black cape with long, bloody teeth, who went around Lovell House blowing out lamps to get himself in the mood to do other, even more terrible things.

Gib, who knew Elmer pretty well by that time, listened to the whole story, thinking that he'd have been scared too if he hadn't heard some of Elmer's tall tales before. But then, when Elmer was about to run down and poor old Rabbit looked to be about to die of suffocation, Gib walked over to the table and took the lid off the lamp's kerosene well.

"Well, now," he said in a loud voice, "if that old ghost had just waited a second before he blew out this here lamp, he might have saved himself the trouble. This thing is plum empty. The wick's all right but the well is bone dry. Come here, Georgie, and take a look."

Miss Mooney came in about then and everybody went back to his own bed and got ready to say his prayers. When prayers were over, Miss Mooney reminded them that silence had begun and then she went around turning off all the lamps except for the small night-light near the door. When she got to the lamp near Georgie's bed she looked around and asked if someone had blown it out.

It was Gib who answered. "No ma'am," he said. "Nobody blew it out. I guess it just ran out of kerosene."

Miss Mooney checked the well, nodded, smiled at Gib, and went on out. And then, when the door closed and the huge room was dark and still, Gib broke the silence rule and said, "No sir, Georgie. Nobody and *no ghost* blew out that lamp. And don't you forget it."

There were a lot of halfway-smothered snickers before everybody went to sleep and forgot all about Elmer's man-eating ghost. As usual, Gib didn't get to sleep right away, but he did stop thinking about Elmer and got back to the latest version of his favorite hope dream. As it turned out later, though, Elmer didn't forget about Gib's taking sides with Georgie and making Elmer Lewis look like a fool.

CHAPTER

4

There were two classrooms at Lovell House, regular classrooms complete with blackboards and real school desks that had slots to hold pens and pencils and, in the right-hand corner, a hole for an ink bottle. Gib had never been to a regular public school, but the boys who had been said the desks looked just about the same.

Five days a week, from seven to eleven-thirty, every Lovell House boy five years old and up went to school. That was another lucky thing for Lovell House orphans, Miss Mooney said. Some orphans in other institutions had very little schooling or even none at all, which, according to Miss Mooney, meant that later in life they would never be able to make anything of themselves.

Sometimes Jacob, who hated school a lot, said he never did know what to make of himself, and if learning to do long division was what it took, he never was going to.

But Gib didn't mind school all that much; at least he didn't when Miss Mooney was his teacher. He particularly liked the parts about reading and writing. "Reading and writing," he told Jacob, "is a lot more interesting than scrubbing floors and washing pots and pans. And if we didn't have to go to school in the mornings, chore time would last all day, like as not."

Jacob could see the truth in that. "Yeah," he said. "I reckon you're right. 'Cept sometimes chores aren't too bad. Like weeding in the garden in the summertime. I'm pretty good at weeding, but I just can't get the hang of reading. It's easy for you. I remember how last year, when you first came, you took to it real quick. Like maybe you been to school before?"

Gib knew it was a question, but he didn't know the answer. He was pretty sure he'd never been in a schoolroom before he came to Lovell House, but he could recall how the letters started right in making themselves into words for him, without his even knowing how he knew. He was pretty fair at spelling too. And that was one reason he'd known for sure that Elmer had been lying when he claimed Gib wrote a dirty word on his spelling test.

It wouldn't have happened if Miss Mooney had been giving the spelling test that day. In the first place, Miss Mooney probably wouldn't have fallen for Elmer's trick, and even if she did, she might have settled things herself instead of putting anybody on report.

But it was Miss Berger, a nervous, twitchy part-time

teacher with a delicate, ladylike voice, who was giving the second-grade spelling test that morning. "And just for today, gentlemen," she said in her highfalutin voice, "we will write the test in pencil rather than ink."

Gib had to smile a little, remembering how the last time she had taught the class she'd been showing how easy it was to use an ink pen, and the sharp old nib stuck into the paper and spattered ink all over her frilly white blouse. So he hadn't really blamed Miss Berger for letting the test be written in pencil, even though that was what got him into such a mess of trouble.

When the test was over, Miss Berger had everybody exchange papers before she read off the correct spellings. "It's not that I would even imagine that any of you would erase your own mistakes," she said, fluttering her ladylike hands. "I refuse to believe that any Lovell House boy would resort to such evil behavior. It's just that I've found that exchanging papers does make for more careful correcting."

Which was probably true. Like as not, Miss Berger really didn't believe that any Lovell House boy would erase his own mistakes. Particularly since she knew that their pencils didn't have erasers. But what she didn't know, and what Gib himself had forgotten for the moment, was that Elmer Lewis had one. A big, square reddish one he'd lifted off a new boy just a few days before.

Gib didn't exchange with Elmer. Even though he had just turned seven at the time and was still pretty much of a Lovell House greenhorn, he wasn't as dumb as all that.

Particularly not after he'd spoiled Elmer's fun by keeping Georgie Olson from dying of fright. But after Gib's paper wound up with Frankie Elsworth, Elmer managed to get Frankie to exchange again.

The test words were all about farming that day. Words like *barn* and *plow* and *horse* and *chicken* and *duck* and *pig*. Gib liked words about farming and he was pretty sure he'd spelled them all right. But when Miss Berger asked for the papers to be handed in, Elmer raised his hand and asked if he could show her something.

Gib knew right away that Elmer was up to no good, because of the look on his face. A phony sorry-faced look, like he'd pulled when Miss Mooney caught him picking the wings off flies and he'd excused himself by saying he hated doing it but felt he ought to because flies were mean, dirty critters. Gib couldn't hear what Elmer whispered to the teacher that day, but Jacob, whose desk was closer, heard the whole thing.

"Ma'am," Elmer whispered, "I just thought you ought to know the kind of words Gibson's been using lately."

According to Jacob, Miss Berger looked downright shocked when she saw what Elmer was pointing to. Too shocked to let Gib tell her what had really happened or even to take another look at the paper. Not even when he tried to point out the brownish red smear where one letter had been erased and written over. And the first thing Miss Berger said, as soon as she quit blushing and fluttering enough to say anything, was that Gibson Whittaker was on report.

CHAPTER

5

Every Lovell House boy knew about being put on report. So everyone in Miss Berger's spelling class knew that as soon as chore time was over, Gib Whittaker would have to come back to Miss Berger's room and then be taken to the headmistress's office. What might happen after that varied according to who was telling it, but it was generally agreed that Gib would at least get a good scolding by Mrs. Hansen, and then probably he'd be sent to bed without any supper.

Gib didn't much like the thought of missing supper, but except for that, he wasn't too upset. Not right at first, anyway. He'd never been on report before, and actually he was kind of curious to see what it would be like. New experiences were pretty hard to come by at Lovell House, and being put on report was at least something out of the ordinary. And besides, he had a feeling that old Mrs. Hansen, who had been headmistress practically forever, was pretty fair-minded and sensible. Too sensible to go all red and fluttery and refuse to even take a close look at a dirty word to see if it had been erased and written over.

"I'll bet Mrs. Hansen will see those eraser marks," Gib told Jacob. "So I can't see how she could blame me. I mean, after she hears about Elmer swiping the eraser and all."

Jacob was worried, though. During chore time, while he and Gib were in the pantry peeling a wheelbarrowful of potatoes that some farmer had donated to the orphanage, Jacob couldn't seem to think about anything else. "What if you get sent to the Repentance Room?" he kept asking Gib.

"I don't know," Gib said, shrugging. "What if? What's supposed to happen in there, anyway?"

Jacob widened his pale blue eyes. "I dunno for sure. Something awful, I guess. No junior's ever been there, far as I know. And not many seniors either, at least not for a long time. Buster says Mrs. Hansen used to send some of the big guys there, but she pretty much quit after something real bad happened."

"Real bad?" Gib asked, and Jacob nodded, rolling out his under lip significantly.

"Bad as can be, I guess," Jacob said. "Buster said some kid had an attack while he was locked up there and when they went to find him he was a goner."

"A goner?" Gib whispered.

"Yep. Dead as a doornail," Jacob said. "And anyways,

30

Mrs. Hansen stopped sending boys up there after that. But just lately it's been happening again."

"Just lately?" Gib cut the last bad spot off the potato he was peeling, dropped it in the bucket, and reached for another.

Jacob nodded. "Yep. That's what Buster says, anyways."

"Yeah? Well, I reckon it's true, then," Gib said. Buster, who at fifteen was Lovell House's oldest resident, was an accepted authority on everything about Lovell House.

"Anyway, the whole thing is just no fair, Gib." Jacob was working himself up into a twitchy, red-faced anger fit. "It's just no fair to get put on report for doing something you didn't do." He bunched his thick blond eyebrows into a bristly scowl, sighed angrily, and threw a potato into the bucket of water so hard it splashed them both.

"Hey, look out," Gib said, glancing over to where Mrs. Romer, the crabbiest of Lovell House's cooks, was shoving chunks of firewood into one of the ranges. "You'll be repenting too if you don't watch out."

After Jacob finally hushed, Gib went back to keeping his mind off *reporting* and *repenting* by thinking about potatoes. About how many potatoes he and Jacob had finished, and how many were still left to be peeled, and which of them was the faster peeler. But concentrating on potatoes only brought to mind the soup Mrs. Romer was getting ready to make, and the fact that nice thick potato soup was one of his favorite suppers. Realizing that he might miss out on potato soup because of Elmer's dirty trick, he was suddenly right on the edge of getting angry enough to make his stomach ache. But then Jacob started in again.

"Lookee here, Gib." This time Jacob's whisper squeaked with excitement. "I just got this great idea. Maybe you could cut yourself real good and . . ." He swished his knife hand in the air, just missing his own fingers. "See, like that. If you give yourself a good enough whack to bloody up some potatoes, Cook might send you to Miss Mooney to get bandaged up. And if you asked her to, I bet she'd tell Miss Berger you were hurt so bad you had to go straight up to bed."

But Gib just laughed and said he'd never heard anything about being on report, or even being sent to the Repentance Room, that made it bad enough to be worth losing blood over. Then, nodding toward where Mrs. Romer was regarding them suspiciously, he added out of the corner of his mouth, "Besides, Cook's watching us. You better just shut up and peel."

A couple of hours later, when the potatoes were all peeled and the soup was starting to smell wonderful, the time came for Gib to report back to Miss Berger. On the way upstairs he'd been thinking about trying one last time to get her to look at the eraser marks, but as soon as he saw her face and the way she picked up his test paper like it was something nasty, he gave up. Except for a couple of sideways glances, they walked all the way to the headmistress's office without even looking at each other.

The office was a large room with a marble fireplace, tall, narrow windows, and, in the center of the room, a big desk with an enormous chair behind it. The woman sitting in the big chair was Mrs. Hansen, all right, but for a moment Gib wasn't entirely sure. In the year and a half he'd been at Lovell House he'd seen the headmistress many times. A tiny figure in a long, dark skirt and high-necked blouse, saying grace in the dining room or visiting classes, she'd always seemed small and wispy to be such an important person—but now she seemed to have shriveled away to almost nothing. Although he'd heard that Mrs. Hansen had been poorly lately, Gib wasn't prepared for the change. He was trying to keep his face from showing his surprise when he became aware of Miss Berger's jittery voice saying, "I'm sorry to bother you about this, ma'am, but I was just so shocked I couldn't think what else . . ."

Miss Berger's voice trailed off as she brought out Gib's spelling paper, unfolded it daintily with the tips of her fingers, and spread it out on the desk. "There it is, ma'am," she said, pointing and blushing. "There, plain as day, on Gibson's spelling test. I just can't tell you what a shock it was. Never in my whole life—"

"Yes, yes. I see." Mrs. Hansen's voice was weak, but it still had a no-nonsense, headmistressy sound to it. "Thank you, Miss Berger. We'll handle this now. You may leave if you wish."

Until Miss Berger had fluttered out the door, Gib's attention had been so concentrated on Mrs. Hansen that he'd been only vaguely aware of the other person in the room. Although he'd seen her only once or twice, he knew it was the new teacher, Miss Offenbacher. A tall, top-heavy woman, with thick braids that coiled around her large face like fat gray snakes, Miss Offenbacher was the sort of person who stayed in your mind, like a chunk of something dry and painful that sticks in your throat no matter how hard you try to swallow.

According to Miss Mooney, Miss Offenbacher had come to Lovell House to teach history and mathematics, and to help in the office until Mrs. Hansen felt better. And Miss Mooney also said that Miss Offenbacher was a fine teacher and Lovell House was lucky to get her.

Miss Mooney had told the truth—as far as she knew, anyway. Gib had heard some things from the older boys about their new teacher, and he could see for himself how Miss Offenbacher was helping out in the office: helping Mrs. Hansen decide what should happen to Gibson Whittaker for letting Elmer Lewis get ahold of his spelling test.

As Gib sidled closer to the desk he could see his test right there in front of Mrs. Hansen. And he could also see, plain as day, the rubbery marks that Elmer's eraser had left behind. He wanted to point out the marks and say how he'd seen Elmer take the new kid's eraser, but the moment he started to talk Miss Offenbacher cut him off.

Sounding shocked and angry, she said, "Just a moment, young man. You will wait to speak until you are asked." So Gib backed off and waited—and waited some more. But nobody ever asked him anything.

Instead Miss Offenbacher went on jabbing her finger at the spelling test and whispering in Mrs. Hansen's ear. Gib didn't hear everything she said, but when Miss Offenbacher finally finished, Mrs. Hansen leaned her head against the chair's high back, closed her eyes, and said in a worn-out voice, "Yes, I'm sure you're right, Miss Offenbacher." She opened her eyes briefly, looked at Gib, and went on. "Do as you see fit."

And so Gib, instead of just missing out on the potato soup, did as Miss Offenbacher saw fit, and paid his first visit to the Repentance Room.

CHAPTER

6

All the way up the three flights of stairs, grand marble, shiny hardwood, and then the narrow, creaky flight that led to the fourth floor, Miss Offenbacher kept a firm grip on Gib's shoulder. A hard, tight hold, as if she was expecting him to try to break away and make a run for it.

To tell the truth, it probably wouldn't even have crossed Gib's mind to run if the grip on his shoulder hadn't made it clear that he was expected to. But even after he thought about it, he didn't come close to trying. For one thing, he couldn't think of anyplace to run to, and for another, he was still hoping he could get the new teacher to listen about the erasure marks. But every time he started, "About Elmer Lewis, ma'am, he—" and then, more desperately, "Ma'am, ma'am. I wasn't the one who—" she only made a sharp hushing noise and tightened her grip.

So, except for a few chopped-off syllables and some tight-lipped hisses, nothing was said before they reached the entrance to the Repentance Room.

The first thing Gib noticed was the sign on the door. In fancy curlicued letters on shiny new paper it said, *Except ye repent ye shall perish.* And the padlock and hasp on the door looked new, too. Taking a key out of her pocket, Miss Offenbacher opened the padlock, shoved back the hasp, and nodded for Gib to go inside. And when he hung back a little she gave him a hard push.

"All right, ma'am, I'm going," Gib said, grabbing the door frame and trying to talk as fast as he could. "But I just want to tell you—"

The clawlike grip again fastened itself on Gib's shoulder and angry red blotches appeared on Miss Offenbacher's long, rawboned face. Her voice tightened into a stutter as she said, "Young man, it's obvious to me that what you've b-b-been wanting to do is to add to your s-s-s-sins. To add lying and t-tattling to your use of filthy language." Gib staggered backward, the door slammed shut, and the key rasped in the lock.

Inside the Repentance Room there was nothing but deep, solid darkness. Darker than midnight in winter and—Gib soon discovered—almost as cold. Clutching his arms around his chest and closing his eyes to blind himself to their uselessness, he sank slowly down to a squatting position and stayed that way until at last the cramping cold forced him to move. Forced him to stand up, shake one stiff leg and then the other, and then, as he stretched out his arms, discover that the walls were surprisingly near.

The Repentance Room was no bigger than a large closet. A storage room for linens, perhaps, from which the shelves had been removed so that the entire space was bare and empty, except for what felt like a kind of pad or carpet on the floor. Kneeling down, Gib ran his fingers over the floor covering and decided that it was a small braided rug.

The exploration didn't take long but somehow it helped a little, as if the worst part had been not knowing what was around him in the darkness and being afraid to find out. But then, when he'd checked out all four walls, there was nothing left to do except wait—and think. Think about what had happened, and what might happen next. Crouched again on the rug with his shoulders hunched against the cold, Gib very soon decided that under the circumstances, thinking about certain subjects only made matters worse.

It was particularly bad, for instance, to do too much thinking about Elmer Lewis, because being really angry had always done uncomfortable things to Gib's stomach. And at the moment his hungry, growling stomach had enough problems without asking for more.

Another thing not to think about, he decided early on, was breathing. The air in the Repentance Room had a dusty, closed-off feel to it, along with a faint whiff of something really bad-smelling, as if a long time ago some Repentance Room prisoner had been so scared that they'd up and . . . But that was as far as he wanted to go with that line of thought.

It was a good bit later, while he was trying not to think about how Miss Offenbacher had told him to wait to speak until he'd been asked, and then never asked him, that Gib suddenly realized he'd forgotten about what he was supposed to be doing. Repenting. He knew, of course, what the word meant. It was a subject that came up pretty often in Lovell House Sunday school classes. But none of the words he remembered seemed to fit very well. For instance, the ones about asking for forgiveness for "what I have done and what I have left undone" didn't make a whole lot of sense when you weren't the one who'd done it. But he decided to give it a try anyway.

Kneeling down on the smelly rug, Gib asked God to forgive him for what he had done. Especially for being dumb enough to let Elmer Lewis get ahold of his spelling test. But as for the next part about what he had left undone, the only thing he could think of was what he had so far left undone to Elmer. So, just to be on the safe side, he also asked for forgiveness for what he might do to Elmer later if he got a chance.

Although he stayed on his knees for quite a while, nothing else came to mind except a lot of things he could always feel real sorry about when he let himself. Like being awful sorry, for instance, that he'd forgotten pretty much everything about where he came from and who he used to belong to.

Thinking about not belonging always seemed to make

a painful thickening in Gib's throat. And the lump got even bigger if he let himself think about how unlikely it was that he'd ever be part of a family again.

He'd been having hope dreams about being part of a real family for a long time by then, but lately it had been getting harder to believe that it might really happen someday. At least not while he was still a junior. The problem was that although Lovell House boys got adopted all the time, not many of them were taken from Junior Hall. Babies were taken from the Infant Room quite often, and once in a while older boys were chosen from among the seniors. Nobody, it seemed, was interested in four- to eight-year-olds. He didn't know why that should be, but it certainly seemed to be true.

There were times, though, when he needed his dreams enough to pretend he still believed in them, and this looked to be one of them. So after shutting off the unbelieving part of his mind he curled himself up on the rag rug and tried to follow Miss Mooney's instructions about picturing everything you hoped for as clearly as you possibly could.

But as time crept slowly by, and the cold deepened in Gib's bones, and hunger growled and scratched at his stomach, it was easier just to feel sorry. Sorry for a poor orphan who had no one to worry about him or even remember where he was. No one to care if he was left forever in a freezing cold closet, until there was nothing left of him except maybe some bones and a new rotten smell oozing up out of the old rug.

But finally, just when he'd convinced himself it would never happen, there was a sound from the stairs. Hobbling, uneven footsteps, the grate of a key in the lock, a burst of light, and there was Buster Gray with a lamp in one hand and a bunch of keys in the other. At that moment, scruffy old Buster with his big ugly ears, pale blotchy skin, and crippled foot was the best-looking person Gib had ever seen.

CHAPTER

7

It took a bit for it to sink in. It wasn't until Buster said, "Okay, jailbird. You want out, or you just going to go on sitting there blinking like a big old owl?" that Gib realized it was really true. He hadn't been forgotten after all. Someone had sent Buster to let him out. Staggering to his feet, he lurched through the door, grabbing his rescuer and almost knocking the lamp out of his hand.

"Hey, take it easy," Buster said. Backing up, he put the lamp down a safe distance away and came back to take hold of Gib's shoulders and turn his face toward the light. "You all right, kid?"

"Boy, am I glad to see you." Gib's openmouthed surprise had turned into his ordinary widemouthed grin.

Buster looked surprised. "Well, what do you know? Looks as how you're doing all right after all. I was figuring to scrape up the pieces this time for sure."

Gib managed a shaky laugh. "Nope. No pieces," he said. "Not now anyways. I'm"—he gulped, gulped again, and went on—"I'm fine now." But when he looked back into the dark hole beyond the Repentance Room door, he couldn't stop the deep shiver that snuck up his spine and jittered in his voice. "But let's g-g-get out of here. Okay?" He started for the stairs, and, picking up the lamp, Buster slowly followed.

Buster never had been speedy because of his crippled foot, but that night, with the heavy lamp to carry, he seemed to be as slow as a big old snail. Right at first Gib tried to match his pace to Buster's, but before long the relief of being free, of having the Repentance Room over and done with, was too much, and on their way down the long hall he must have kicked up his heels a little, like a colt put out to pasture. Buster was chuckling when they got to the door of Junior Hall.

"What's funny?" Gib whispered.

Buster was still smiling as he said, "You are, kid. You are one tough little . . ."

Gib didn't hear the last word. "Tough little what?" he asked.

Buster shrugged. "Junior," he said. "I said one tough little junior."

"Hey." Gib grabbed the older boy's arm and whispered, "Buster, I been wondering. How come juniors don't get adopted?"

Buster frowned. "What do you mean?" he asked. "No law against it, far as I know."

"I know," Gib said. "But they don't very often, do they? Infants do, and seniors sometimes, but not—"

"Shhh!" Buster put his finger to his lips and nodded toward the door to the dormitory. "It's silence time. Remember?" And then, when Gib let his disappointment show, he added, "Later, kid. You'll find out all about it later."

Inside the dormitory there was silence and, except in the night lamp's small circle, a far-reaching, overlapping jungle of shadows. But at least here in the hall the darkness was a bit warmer, and the smell, a musty mix of polished woodwork, dirty socks, and bed wetters' mattresses, was comfortingly familiar. Gib moved forward eagerly. At cot number nine he was taking off his shoes when he heard an approaching rustle and then a quavering whisper. "Gib? That you? You all right?"

"Hey, Jacob," Gib whispered back. "You still awake?"

A barefooted, nightshirted shadow moved against the deeper, more distant dark, and Jacob whispered indignantly, " 'Course I am. I haven't closed my eyes once." As he moved cautiously forward, Jacob's whisper became even more accusing. "Holy moley, Gib. What did they do to you? I been waiting and waiting. Must be almost midnight. Here." He stuck out a hand, which, in the darkness, thumped into Gib's chest.

Gib staggered back, grinning. "Hey, I'm sorry. Take it easy," he said. Then the fist came again and opened on the remains of a dried-out slice of bread. "Saved it for you," Jacob was whispering, when Gib suddenly noticed that he and Jacob weren't the only ones awake. All around them there were rustling sounds and tiny glints of light, the reflected shine of the night lamp in many wide-open eyes. And Gib and Jacob weren't the only ones out of bed, either. By now there were five, maybe six, other boys moving toward bed number nine. Shuffling nervously on cold, bare feet, they surrounded Gib and shoved things into his hands. Bread, mostly, but also a partly eaten apple and even a small chunk of half-cooked potato.

"Was it just terrible, Gib?" The shadow with the whimpery whisper was Bobby Whitestone, for sure. "Did she whip you real hard?"

"Naw." Trying to swallow a mouthful of dry bread and cold potato, Gib managed to say, "What makes you think I got whipped?"

"Daniel said you do. When Daniel got sent to the Repentance Room he got whipped real hard."

"That right?" Gib was still mumbling—and chewing. "Maybe you only get whipped if you steal something."

There was a "yeah, maybe" and several nodding heads. According to Junior Hall gossip, Daniel, a senior who worked in the kitchen, had stolen some cheese from the staff's pantry.

"But what *was* it like, Gib?" Bobby's voice was tense and urgent.

So Gib told them how it was nothing but a big closet

without any shelves, with an old rag rug on the floor. When he finished, there were shocked, disbelieving whispers.

"But Daniel says it's haunted," someone hissed, " 'cause somebody died there."

"Haunted?" Gib was asking when someone muttered, "Shhh. Listen. Somebody's coming."

The hasty shuffle of feet and the creak of cots had barely died away when the door opened and Miss Mooney came in carrying a night lantern. For a moment she stood in the doorway before she moved softly down the aisle to stop at the foot of Gib's bed. Gib made his breathing deep and steady, and after a moment Miss Mooney turned away and went back down the aisle to the hall door.

A few minutes later most of the pretend deep breathing had settled into something steadier. But not Gib's. Gib was still wide awake without knowing why—except part of it might have been that he wasn't ready to risk having a Repentance Room nightmare.

But there was more to it than that. The other part was about Jacob and the others who'd saved him something from their skimpy suppers and maybe a dozen more who'd stayed awake to see how he was. And then too, there was Elmer to think about.

Suddenly Gib sat up and looked down the aisle past one, two, three deep-breathing, gray-blanketed cocoons, to the one that was Elmer Lewis. And then, right while Gib was staring, the Elmer cocoon stirred, flopped restlessly, and raised up on one elbow. For a part of a second they stared at each other, before Elmer flopped back down and jerked his blanket up over his head.

Gib couldn't help chuckling out loud. Loud enough for Elmer to hear, probably, but the chuckle wasn't just to be ornery. Part of it was something about the way old Elmer ducked for cover like a cottontail who'd spotted a coyote. As he lay back down Gib was imagining sneaking over and doing a coyote howl right next to old Elmer's ear, and he might have really done it if he hadn't been so tired. The next thing he knew it was morning.

CHAPTER

8

That year, the year Gib Whittaker turned nine years old, was a time of many changes, and not only for him. The first and biggest change was the new headmistress. There had been rumors for some time that Mrs. Hansen was very sick, so the formal announcement of her death—of her passing over to Glory, as Mr. Garrison put it—didn't come as a complete surprise. The announcement was made by Mr. T. Everett Garrison during a special assembly on a Sunday afternoon in September. Mr. Garrison, who had introduced himself as the president of the Lovell House board, gave a long talk about what a wonderful headmistress Mrs. Hansen had been, and then he made another announcement—that the board had already chosen a new headmistress. Before the boys were dismissed to go back to their quarters, the president of the board asked everyone to pray for Mrs.

Hansen's soul, and also for Miss Offenbacher's success in her role as the new headmistress of Lovell House.

All during Mr. Garrison's long speech Gib kept wondering how some grown-ups could talk for so long about something important without telling you anything you really needed to know. There were a lot of questions Gib was dying to ask, but he was pretty sure he wouldn't get a chance to. Mr. Garrison, a slope-shouldered gentleman with a busy, thin-lipped mouth, didn't look like the type to answer questions. Finally Gib gave up on getting any answers and fell back on admiring the way Mr. Garrison never slowed down when he ran out of anything to say, and just carried on by using some of his fanciest phrases over and over again. Answers could wait, Gib decided, until they were back in Junior Hall with Miss Mooney.

As it turned out, Gib wasn't the only one who had some questions for Miss Mooney. But for once, even Miss Mooney wasn't great about answering. At least not right at first, when, once they were back in the hall, some thirty boys clustered around her, frantically waving their hands to be called on.

Instead of calling on anybody, the first thing Miss Mooney did was to tell them to bow their heads and ask God's blessing on Mrs. Hansen's soul. And after they'd all done that she went on asking for more prayers and blessings. Blessings on everybody at Lovell House and pretty much all over the world. So they all prayed together, repeating the words after Miss Mooney as hard and fast as they could, each one hurrying to get to the "amen" so he could be the first one to raise his hand again.

Finally Miss Mooney sighed, wiped her eyes with her handkerchief, and started calling on the most desperately waving hands, and of course one of the first was Bobby Whitestone's. Bobby's question was a desperate one all right. What he wanted to know was what had killed Mrs. Hansen, and if it was catching, because if it was, he was sure to get it next. It wasn't until Miss Mooney promised Bobby that Mrs. Hansen didn't die of anything catching that he began to calm down a little.

Next she called on one of the youngest juniors, a little five-year-old named Jonah, who'd been crying quietly all during the prayers. Jonah didn't exactly have a question, though. What Jonah wanted was for Miss Mooney to promise that she wasn't going to die, too.

Miss Mooney seemed to have a hard time answering most of the questions. Particularly when she had to talk about Mrs. Hansen.

Mrs. Hansen, she said, died mostly of old age, and she was going to be terribly, terribly missed by everyone at Lovell House. Then she asked them to give her a moment to compose herself, so they did, but as soon as she'd wiped her eyes they all started in again.

Herbie Watson asked if Miss Offenbacher was sick, too, and if that was why she had to be prayed for, and dumb old Frankie asked what kind of a board Mr. Garrison was president of. Like, did it have to be some real special kind of board, or would an ordinary old plank do?

Gib could tell that Miss Mooney was having a hard time answering all the questions, so he decided to wait until later to ask his. Particularly since his first one was the kind she might not want to answer in front of everybody. His first, and most important, question was why Miss Mooney wasn't going to be the new headmistress, instead of Miss Offenbacher.

And the second one wouldn't be easy, either. It was the one he'd been waiting to ask for a long time, about whether there was some kind of a rule against allowing Junior Hall boys to be adopted.

So he didn't get to ask either of his questions that day, but about a week later one of them answered itself when a Junior Hall boy got adopted after all.

It happened one day at breakfast—at least the only part Gib got to see, happened then. He had almost finished his oatmeal when he heard Miss Offenbacher's voice and looked up in time to see her come into the dining hall with a tall man dressed in a long, dusty black overcoat. The tall stranger had a large nose, a stringy dark gray beard, and deep-set, flickery eyes.

Instead of introducing the stranger and asking everyone to say hello, the way Mrs. Hansen had always done when a possible adoptive parent came to visit, Miss Offenbacher just led the way up and down the aisles, stopping now and then and asking a boy to stand up and say hello to Mr. Bean. Afterward, when he knew more about the man, Gib shivered when he remembered how he and Jacob had grinned at each other about the name. "Bean?" Gib mouthed, and Jacob mouthed back, "Beanpole."

Miss Offenbacher led the man named Bean through the seniors first, but then, when the visitor pointed, she started down the first table of juniors.

The first boy at the juniors' table was fat old Fred MacDonald, but the visitor just shook his head and went on. Gib was next. He'd been planning what he'd do if he ever had a chance to meet someone who'd come to adopt. He'd even practiced it now and then, when no one was looking. Practiced standing up straight and showing his teeth in a big smile—Miss Mooney had told him he had a good smile—and speaking out clearly if he was asked any questions. So he stood up quickly and smiled, even though he was already beginning to feel that there was something about the visitor that made a smile hard to come by.

But the man only nodded and moved on, and on, until he came to, of all people, wheezy little rabbit-faced Georgie Olson. And then, after Georgie had stammered out his name, "George Olson," and his age, "Almost nine, sir," the black-coated man nodded at Miss Offenbacher, turned on his heel, and tromped out of the room. And then she left too, right after she'd told Georgie to report to her office as soon as the bell rang for classes.

Gib always remembered Georgie's face that day as he

left the dining room. The usual Georgie was there, the nervous, jumpy, rabbity one, but there was something new, too. Some little bit of hopefulness, maybe, and even a little bit of pride that out of all the juniors he'd been the one chosen.

And sure enough, by the next day Georgie was gone. Scared little rabbit-faced Georgie Olson had been adopted.

CHAPTER

9

Of course there was a lot of talk in Junior Hall in the days that followed Georgie's adoption. Talk and wishful thinking and a certain amount of envy. At least Gib felt a little bit that way, picturing Georgie living in a real house with the kind of family Gib's daydreams had created. A farming family in a big, shady, everlasting kind of house out in the country, with a bunch of kids and lots of horses and other animals. But Jacob didn't agree. Jacob said he was glad he hadn't been chosen.

"Me? Me wish that old Billy Whiskers had picked me?" he said when Gib asked him. "Not on your tin-type."

"Why not?" Gib asked. "Don't you ever want to live with a family like a normal person?"

Jacob shrugged. "Sure I do," he said. "Someday, maybe. But that old geezer had a mean look about him."

Gib nodded reluctantly. "Yeah, I know. But

maybe . . ." He paused, not wanting to admit his own reaction to the man who had taken poor Georgie. "But could be he's better than he looks. You know. Handsome is . . . ," he began, and Jacob laughed and joined in to finish one of Miss Mooney's favorite quotes. ". . . as handsome does."

"Anyway, he picked a junior," Gib said. "That proves there's no law against it. So maybe one of us will get picked next time."

Jacob snorted. "Well, they'll have to show up pretty soon," he said. "To get ahold of us while we're still juniors."

Jacob was right about that. In October Jacob passed his ninth birthday and moved upstairs, and a couple of months later Gib followed. So they left behind forever the huge old ballroom with its thirty-some childish occupants, and joined sixteen older boys in the smaller hall on the third floor. And it very soon became obvious to Gib that Buster Gray hadn't been fooling when he said that a senior's life wasn't exactly easy.

Just as Buster had warned, the upstairs hall was cold and drafty. And the chores assigned senior boys were certainly harder, most of the heavy mopping and scrubbing indoors, and all the outdoor stuff in cold weather. But worst of all, seniors were taught by different instructors. Instead of Miss Mooney and Miss Berger, they were now housemothered by Miss Offenbacher herself. And taught, too, at least until Mr. Harding showed up.

A thick-chested man, with a bushy beard and a shiny

bald head, Mr. Harding had been hired when Miss Offenbacher began to spend most of her time in the headmistress's office. When he first heard about the new teacher, Gib, as well as most of the other senior boys, had been pleased, or at least a little relieved. First of all, it might be interesting having a man teacher for a change. And second, the new man would have to be pretty bad to be worse than you know who.

Gib went on trying to feel that way even after Mr. Harding started his first day by introducing his best friend. Mr. Harding's best friend turned out to be a wide, flat board with a handle on one end. His friend's name was Mr. Paddle, he said, and Mr. Paddle was going to be their friend, too, by helping them all to become excellent students and good, law-abiding citizens.

On that first day Mr. Harding didn't go on to explain just how Mr. Paddle was going to be so helpful, but Gib had an uncomfortable feeling he already knew. And during chore time that same afternoon, he found out that some of the other boys had the same feeling.

"Shucks," Jacob said when Gib asked him, "everybody knowed what he meant. And what's more, he knowed that we knowed." Dropping his snow shovel, Jacob pretended to whack Gib on the backside with an imaginary Mr. Paddle. "That's how," Jacob grunted between whacks. "He meant he's going to beat the tar out of us if we don't do to suit him."

They were halfway down the orphanage's curving driveway at the time, trying to clean up after a medium-sized blizzard that had raged all night and most of the morning. Six senior boys, shoveling and shivering in their thin overcoats and frazzled-out mittens, trying to clear a passageway wide enough for the orphanage buggy and any Lovell House visitors that might happen to show up.

"Yeah, that's what I thought, too," Gib said between shovelfuls of the heavy, wet snow. Then he stopped long enough to poke Jacob with the handle of his shovel. "Lucky us, huh?"

Jacob laughed and poked back, and all the other shovelers stopped to look at Gib and Jacob expectantly. So they both did their famous dumb-but-happy faces that everybody looked for whenever anybody mentioned the word *lucky*. Looked and fell apart laughing, or, when the situation made laughing too dangerous, tried their best not to look.

The situation at that particular moment hadn't seemed especially dangerous. Except for the six of them, Gib, Jacob, Luke, Frankie, Abner, and Fred, no one else was in sight and the front windows of Lovell House were a long way away and pretty well frosted over. But the way it turned out, somebody must have been looking, because an hour or so later, when the six of them were in the coatroom cleaning up, Buster came in and handed Gib and Jacob report slips.

"Report?" Jacob squealed. "Where? To who?"

Buster sighed and shook his head. "Harding," he said. "Harding's classroom. Soon as you get cleaned up."

That was the day Gib and Jacob made the acquaintance of Mr. Paddle. On their way upstairs they tried to reassure each other that they had nothing to worry about.

"What did we do, for heaven's sake?" Jacob said. "I mean, we did the lucky face thing and everybody laughed some, but there was no way anyone could've seen that. Was there? You see how anybody could have seen us, Gib?"

Gib agreed. "Leastways not unless they rubbed some frost off a window first." He put an evil expression on his face and pantomimed the rubbing and peering, and Jacob did manage a weak grin. But when they reached the senior classroom they could tell immediately that they had nothing to grin about. When they walked into the classroom Mr. Harding was in his shirtsleeves, and Mr. Paddle was lying right there on his desk.

"Sir," Gib said hurriedly when, without a word, Mr. Harding picked up the paddle and headed in his direction. "Sir, could you tell us what we did? I mean, so we'll know not to do it again."

Afterward, back in the dorm, Gib and Jacob told an audience of eight or ten other seniors about what happened. "And then old Harding kind of chuckled in that nasty way of his," Jacob said. " 'Huh! Huh! Huh!' And he pushed Gib down across a desk and lit into him with the paddle. 'I—think—you—know.' " Jacob went on being Mr. Harding, showing how he swatted with every word. " 'And if—you—don't—Mr. Paddle will—teach you.' "

Frankie Elsworth's face was screwed up like something

58

was hitting him too. "Did it hurt real bad?" he asked in a jittery voice.

Gib was easing himself down onto his cot at the moment and trying not to let his face show what his backside still felt like. But once he was flat down it wasn't too bad. "Naw," he said, grinning at Frankie. "It wasn't too bad."

"It was *bad*!" Jacob shouted. "Real bad. And badder for Gib than for me. Gib got ten whacks and I only got five."

"Why? Why was that, Gib?" Frankie's eyes had the same kind of shamefaced eagerness that he got when people talked dirty. "Why'd you get ten, Gib?"

Gib had to think about that. "I dunno," he said finally. "Probably because I asked what we'd done. Guess that was it." He managed the beginning of a grin. "Yep. I guess that's what Mr. Paddle taught me today. Don't ever ask questions."

But a little later, when they thought Gib had gone to sleep, Jacob told Bobby and Luke something different. "It was because Gib wasn't looking scared enough," Jacob whispered, pulling the other boys away from Gib's cot. "That's what I think, anyway. What I think is, it made old Harding mad when Gib acted so kind of . . . calm and collected like."

"Collected? What you mean by collected, Jacob?"

Jacob sighed impatiently. Impatient with Bobby for asking such a hard question, and impatient with himself for not being able to come up with a better way of explaining what he meant. "You know, dummy," he said

crossly. "Collected means not all scared and jumpy like
. . . Well, take a good look in the mirror, Whitestone,
and you'll know *exactly* what being *un*collected is like."

Bobby got mad at first, which of course was just what
Jacob meant for him to do. But then, after he thought a
while longer, he said, "Yeah, well, if all being collected
gets you is a bunch of extra whacks, I'm just as glad to go
right on being uncollected. So there, Mr. Smart Aleck
Fetters."

But Jacob, who had just finished easing himself down
onto his bed, only groaned a little and pretended to go to
sleep.

CHAPTER

10

Gib hadn't really been asleep, or at least not quite, that afternoon when Jacob said that Gib had made Harding angry by being too "calm and collected." And just like Bobby, Gib was curious about what Jacob meant. Not quite curious enough to admit that he'd been listening under false pretenses, maybe, but enough to give him something to think about besides the ache in his backside. He hadn't finished figuring it out by the time the supper bell rang, but he'd gotten far enough to agree with Bobby that being collected wasn't anything to brag about. At least not if you were nothing but a poor old orphan, with nobody to care if somebody like Mr. Harding decided to make you his favorite punching bag.

In the weeks that followed, Gib had several other meetings with Mr. Harding and his paddle. For whatever reason, whether it was because he was too "collected" or something entirely different, it was becoming obvious that Gib was well on his way to setting some kind of a record for encounters with Mr. Paddle. One night, the evening after Gib's fourth or fifth beating, he and Jacob and Bobby had a discussion on the subject.

"It's just not fair," Bobby said. He was sitting on the foot of Gib's bed at the time, barefooted and in his nightshirt. "You didn't do anything. Not today, or any of the other times, really. At least nothing more than what other people get away with all the time. He just likes pickin' on you."

"Yeah. Sure seems that way." Gib shifted his position, trying to put his weight on a less painful part of his backside. "This time I sure didn't do anything, except maybe smile a little when he broke his old pointer."

The pointer, a piece of wood covered with fancy carvings and shaped something like a drummer's stick was what Mr. Harding used to point to things on maps and the blackboard, and to whack people's knuckles when they messed up an answer to a question. But that morning he'd tried out a new way to use it, and it hadn't worked too well. He'd been working himself up into a real tizzy about people who didn't listen, and all of a sudden he shouted "Attention!" and hit the corner of his desk real hard—and his fancy old pointer almost exploded. Shattered pieces of pointer flew everywhere, and Mr. Harding kind of flinched and muttered something that sounded a lot like the word Elmer had written on Gib's spelling test.

Remembering the expression on Harding's face when

62

the pointer flew apart, Gib's lips did it again before he managed to straighten them out and say solemnly, "But I didn't laugh. Not really."

Jacob agreed with him. "You didn't!" he said. "I was looking, and I saw how hard you didn't." He sighed. "What are you going to do, Gib? Rate you're going, there's not going to be much left of you to beat on by the time you're eighteen."

"Yeah, I know." Grimacing, Gib pushed himself to a sitting position. Firming his chin and narrowing his eyes, he said, "But I'm *not* going to be here that long. I've decided I'm going to get myself adopted. No reason I can't." He gestured around the room, where about a dozen other boys ranging in age from nine to fifteen were getting ready for bed. "Look, there were more than twice as many of us when we were juniors. And now Herbie's adopted, and Albert. And Georgie too, when he wasn't even a senior yet."

"Yeah, I know," Jacob was saying when suddenly he pointed to where Buster Gray had just come in. "Hey, I'm going to ask Buster about it. Bet he'd know."

"Buster," Gib called. "Can you come here a minute? We got to ask you something."

Carrying his night monitor's lantern, Buster limped down the hall and stopped at the foot of Gib's cot. A thin-lipped grin cut across his lopsided face as he looked from Bobby to Jacob and then on to Gib. "What d'you need to know?" he asked Gib. "Can't say for sure I can answer, but I'll give it a try."

"I want to know how to get out of here," Gib said.

Buster looked startled. He started to back away, shaking his head. " 'Fraid I can't help. . . ."

"I don't mean run away," Gib said quickly. "I mean get adopted." He gestured again to the half-empty room. "You know, like Georgie and Herbie and all the rest of them who were here a while back."

Buster still looked worried. He glanced around the room and then sat down on the foot of Gib's cot, pushing Bobby off onto the floor. Lowering his voice almost to a whisper, he said, "Lookee here. I'm not supposed to answer any questions about things like that. Not about any kind of adoption, but . . ." He looked around again. "You promise me you won't tell I told you? Cross your heart and hope to die?"

Gib and Jacob and Bobby looked at each other, nodded solemnly, and crossed their hearts.

Still whispering, Buster said, "They didn't all get adopted, you know. Not all the seniors who left got—"

"We know that," Gib interrupted. "Most of them were only half orphans, so they probably just went home to their pa, or whatever family they got left."

Jacob looked indignant. "Yeah," he said, "like their folks dumped them in an orphanage when they were babies and then decided to take them back after they got old enough to be useful."

"But the full orphans, like us?" Gib's nod included Bobby and Jacob. "And Herbie. He was a full orphan, and so was Georgie. They got adopted, didn't they?"

Buster shook his head. "Not really. What they got was . . ." Buster paused and looked around again before he said, "What they got was farmed out."

"Farmed out?" All three pairs of his listeners' lips formed the words in silent unison.

"That's right. Farmed out," Buster said. Then, lowering his voice again so that they had to strain to hear, "Farmed out means they got signed up for by people, farmers usually, who aren't really looking to adopt at all. All they're looking for is some good cheap labor. Real cheap. No pay at all till you're eighteen and then, if you're lucky, fifty dollars and a suit of new clothes." Buster's face was grim as he went on, "Slave labor for eight, maybe ten years, and then out you go."

There was a longish silence before Jacob said, "Well, heck. What's so bad about that? Same as here almost, 'cept for the fifty dollars. You going to get fifty dollars when you leave here, Buster?"

Buster's grin had a sarcastic look to it. "Not likely," he said. "But here you get something to eat and some schooling and—"

"You mean farmed-out kids don't have to go to school?" Jacob was definitely interested.

"And get starved, maybe?" Bobby whimpered. "Do they get starved, Buster?"

But Buster was getting to his feet. Holding up his lantern, he looked nervously around the room and started to edge away before he whispered, "Not always."

"Not always?" Gib asked. "Not always what?"

"Not always anything," Buster answered. "That's the misery of it. There's no way of knowing what you'll run into when you get farmed out."

"Buster! Buster!" they called after him, but he only stopped long enough to remind them of their promise.

"Remember, don't tell anybody else. Not anyone. And most of all, don't say who told you," he demanded, and when they all nodded he turned and limped hurriedly away on his nighttime rounds.

CHAPTER
11

In the days that followed, the short dark days of a bitterly cold January, Gib spent a lot of time wondering about what Buster had said, even though it was the kind of thinking that always made him miserable. Not just sad and gloomy miserable, either, but angry too, as if someone had lied to him or maybe broken a promise. And he went on feeling that way for a while, even after it came to him that no one had lied about Lovell House adoptions. No one except himself. He himself had made up a lying dream, a hope dream, and dreamt it over and over again until he'd come to depend on it. And losing it left him feeling lost and deserted.

Bobby said they should have known all along. They should have known that nothing good could come of being adopted, and that staying at Lovell House, as bad as it was now that Miss Offenbacher and Mr. Harding

67

were running things, was probably the best they could ever hope for in their whole lives.

But Gib couldn't quite give up hope. "Yeah, yeah, yeah," he said one night when Bobby was being particularly gloomy. "But you gotta remember what Buster said about 'not always.'"

Jacob nodded. "Yeah, I remember. But I'm not sure what he meant. He didn't tell us, and now he probably won't, not ever. He's been acting kind of nervous and jumpy since he told us all that stuff. Like maybe Miss Offenbacher would kick him out if she knew he'd been spilling the beans. When I tried to talk to him the other day he just said, 'Hush up that kind of talk!' and skittered off in a big hurry."

But Gib had thought a lot about what Buster meant about "not always." "I bet I know," he said. "He just meant that being farmed out is not always so bad, or so good either. Just depends on who gets you, I guess."

Gib wanted his guess to be true. If even that much was true, maybe it meant you could go on hoping. Hoping for Herbie and Georgie, and for yourself too, if it should happen to you. Maybe it was enough, Gib told himself, if you could at least go on hoping.

But it was only a few days later, on a Friday near the end of that same mean, bitter January, that Gib found out that hoping wasn't enough. At least not for everyone.

When Mr. Harding read off the chore assignments that morning, Gib and Bobby, just the two of them, had been assigned the job of mucking out the dairy barn and

Juno's box stall. On an ordinary day taking care of the orphanage's buggy horse and two Jersey milk cows was Gib's favorite chore. Of course, shoveling out old, dirty bedding and replacing it with clean straw and sawdust was a lot less fun when the temperature was way below freezing. Particularly when you were shorthanded because half the senior boys were sick with colds and fever.

"Those fakers aren't the only sick ones," Bobby whimpered as he and Gib shoveled endlessly at frozen clumps of cow manure and dirty straw, piled them into a wheelbarrow, and then took turns trundling the barrow way out across the frozen back pasture to the manure pile. "I got me a terrible case of the grippe coming on. I can tell."

Gib threw another shovelful onto the load and then stopped long enough to stare at Bobby. "You getting a sore throat?" he asked.

Bobby swallowed thoughtfully. "Yeah," he agreed. "Real raw like. And a fever too." Yanking off a mitten, he felt his forehead with his bare fingers. "Burning up," he confirmed.

Gib put down his shovel, took off one glove, felt Bobby's face, and shook his head. "Feels pretty cold to me," he said.

"No it don't. Not inside, anyways. Inside I'm just about to burn up."

Gib grinned. "Burning up inside, huh?" Pulling on his glove, he slapped his hands together before he picked up his shovel. "Lucky you. Might keep you from freezing solid on the outside." He'd meant it as a joke, but it sure didn't cheer Bobby up a whole lot. He went right on groaning and sighing as they finished the cow barn, pushed the final wheelbarrow load out of the milking stall, and started to scatter the fresh straw.

Interrupting a particularly mournful sigh, Gib said, "Look here, Bobby. I'll dump the last load." Actually it wasn't his turn, and Bobby knew it. "You go ahead and finish spreading the straw, then take the lantern and shovels over to Juno's stall. I'll be along soon as I dump this one." Grabbing the handles of the wheelbarrow, he headed out across the frozen field to the manure heap.

It had been bad enough in the cow barn, but outside it was worse. A lot worse. The wind-driven sleet beat against Gib's face and seemed to cut directly to the center of his bones. But even with his eyes squinted half shut against the wind, and with a lot of slipping and sliding on the ice-crusted snow, he covered the distance to the manure heap in record time.

Actually he was hurrying for two reasons. Not only to escape from the wind, but also because Juno and her box stall came next, and he liked being around the old chestnut mare. Liked listening to her soft, eager nicker as he fetched her hay and oats, and the smell of her horsey warmth as he brushed her mane and tail and, standing on a grooming stool so he could reach, ran the currycomb down her strong, wide back. He liked the currying and he could tell that Juno did too. And he also liked knowing that for once he wouldn't have to argue with Bobby to get the best job, because Bobby was sure that Juno, like everything else big and powerful, was out to get him.

"She's getting ready to bite me," he'd told Gib at least half a dozen times. "I can tell." Just thinking about Bobby being so scared of gentle old Juno that he'd do all the shoveling while Gib did the fun part made Gib smile, even though stretching his lips made painful prickles across his half-frozen face.

Back inside, out of the storm, Gib was struggling to shove the barn door shut against the push of the wind when Bobby suddenly appeared beside him. A bulgy-eyed Bobby, whose arms flailed wildly in pointless gestures and whose mouth gasped and flapped and made senseless sounds. A threatening shiver started up Gib's back, and something hard and heavy seemed to fall from a great distance and crash into the pit of his stomach.

"What is it?" he asked. "Bobby? What's the matter? You seen a ghost or something?"

Bobby gulped again, grabbed Gib's arm, and turned back to point in the direction of Juno's stall. "Somebody's in there," he gasped. "In the stall. I think it's . . ." He stared at Gib with wide, unbelieving eyes. "It might be— it might be Georgie and . . ." His voice rose to a wail. ". . . and I think he's dead."

It was Georgie Olson all right, or all that was left of him, lying in a filthy, ragged heap in a corner of Juno's stall, where it looked like he'd tried to make a bed for himself of straw and gunnysacks and the torn scraps of an old horse blanket. Had made himself a bed, curled up in it, and was now asleep. Or dead?

"Did Juno kill him?" Bobby was whimpering from outside the stall door. "Look, she's looking at him."

Juno, who was standing quietly on the other side of the stall, was indeed looking at Georgie curiously, her ears pricked forward.

Gib shook his head. "No, 'course not," he said, and, dropping to his knees, he grabbed Georgie's shoulder and shook him. "Georgie," he said, and then more loudly, "come on, Georgie, wake up."

Georgie wasn't dead after all. At least not quite. Suddenly awake, he cowered away from Gib, covering his head and face with his arms and making a strange squeaking noise like an injured animal.

"Hush. Stop that," Gib whispered. "Be still, Georgie. It's just us. Gib and Bobby. We won't hurt you."

The squeaking stopped. Georgie's arms, heavily bandaged like his hands, came down slowly, away from his face. And suddenly Gib was struggling to keep his own face from showing his shock and horror. Georgie was almost unrecognizable. If it hadn't been for his long rabbity upper lip and pale white-lashed blue eyes, Gib might have taken him for a stranger. A stranger whose face had shriveled to a sharp-edged skull except where swollen, scaly patches of frostbite blotched his nose and cheeks.

"Gib? Bobby? Oh, Gib, please help me. Help me hide." Georgie's high-pitched voice quavered tearfully

72

and he reached out toward Gib with both bandaged arms.

Before Gib could respond, Bobby asked, "What happened, Georgie? What's wrong with your hands?"

Georgie looked down at his own outstretched arms and a new kind of horror crept across his face. "They're going to cut them off," he whispered. "Both of them. Mister said they were going to cut off both my hands. So when he stopped at the store I jumped out and ran. I didn't know where to go so I came here and . . ."

"Why?" Gib tried to keep the horror out of his voice. "Why would they cut off your hands?"

Georgie stared at his hands and tried to answer, but at first his chattering teeth and trembling lips blurred the sounds. As his voice steadied, Gib was able to make out what he was saying. ". . . Mister said he'd learn me to take care of my mittens. Said I always lose them, but I don't. The dog took them. I know he did, but Mister wouldn't believe me. He whipped me like always, and then he said I had to do the east pasture anyways. Mittens or no mittens."

Gib shook his head in wonder. "Do the east pasture?" he asked.

Georgie nodded. "Weather like this, he sleds hay out to the stock. Four bales this time, he said. You got to harness the mule and load the hay on the sled and drive way out there and—and . . ." Georgie's voice died away as he stared down at his bandaged hands. "It was so cold the hay hooks stuck to my skin. When I got back my hands was froze. Missus put water on them—it hurt real bad—and then she told Mister he had to take me to the doctor. He said naw, he wouldn't neither. Said I was no good, and he didn't care if I froze solid—but then, when Missus started out to get the buggy, he said, 'All right, goddammit, I'll do it.'

" 'You get on back in the house,' he told Missus. 'I'll take him.' But then, in the buggy, he told me he'd seen hands like mine afore and they'd have to cut them off. Both of them. So, soon as I got the chance, I ran."

Georgie's tears mingled with a yellowish liquid that oozed from the dark, swollen patches on his cheeks and nose. He held out his bandaged hands as if he were praying. "Don't tell on me," he begged. "Please don't tell I'm here."

Gib's own eyes were hot and wet and he couldn't find his voice, but Bobby was saying, "But you can't stay here, Georgie. Someone always comes out to see if we did a good job. Buster comes mostly—but sometimes it's Mr. Harding. He'll see you."

"Yeah." Gib's voice had suddenly returned. He looked around. "Come on, Bobby. We'll make him a bed in the tack room while we finish up here and then—"

"And then *what*? And then what are you planning to do, Whittaker?" The voice was hard and sharp and only too familiar. It belonged to Mr. Harding.

CHAPTER

12

Of course it was Mr. Harding. Gib should have known it would be. It explained why the job of cleaning the barn and stable had been given to a crew of only two boys. Harding knew they wouldn't be able to finish in time. It usually took a three-man crew even in good weather, and during a blizzard it should have been four or five. So the job would be skimped on and that meant that Harding would have another excuse to beat the tar out of somebody. That had been his plan, sure enough, and it might have worked that way except for Georgie Olson's showing up and changing things some.

The next thing Mr. Harding said was that they were all going to Miss Offenbacher's office, immediately. He brushed Bobby aside and opened the stall door, but when he stood over Georgie and said, "All right, kid, on your feet. Get up immediately," nothing much happened. Nothing except that Georgie tried for a long, painful minute, heaving himself up on his elbows and then collapsing again with a pitiful groan.

Mr. Harding didn't offer to carry him. Right at first he made as if he was thinking about it, but when he bent close and got a good look at Georgie's swollen, oozing face and maybe got a whiff of him, he changed his mind. "Get on each side of him and put his arms over your shoulders," he told Gib and Bobby. So they did, but hanging from his arms must have hurt Georgie a lot because by the time they got to the back hallway his head had lolled over sideways and his feet were mostly just dragging. Unconscious, Gib thought, or maybe even dead.

On the way to the office Mr. Harding went ahead, opening doors and waiting for Gib and Bobby to struggle through with the dead weight of Georgie dangling between them. The back hall was empty, but as they made their way into the entryway Gib thought he heard gasps and whispers that seemed to be coming from above, and then the rapidly fading sound of retreating footsteps on the grand stairway.

The office was empty. "Put him there in the armchair," Mr. Harding said as he left the room. "I'll get Miss Offenbacher."

As Gib and Bobby lowered Georgie into the chair his head flopped back helplessly and he slumped sideways over one of the arms.

"Here, you hold him up," Gib whispered. "I'm going—"

"Going?" Bobby wailed. "Where? Don't leave me alone, Gib. Don't!"

At the door Gib looked back long enough to say, "Got to. Got to find Miss Mooney."

"Don't go. Come back," Bobby howled. "What can she do?"

Gib didn't know what Miss Mooney could do. Miss Offenbacher was headmistress, so she had the last say about everything, and both she and Mr. Harding were a whole lot bigger and stronger than Miss Mooney. But Gib felt sure that if Georgie had any chance at all, it would be because of Miss Mooney. Running full speed across the entry hall and up the grand staircase, he bolted down the second floor hallway, past the entrance to Junior Hall, to the door of Miss Mooney's private room. But no one answered his first knock or even, a moment later, his frantic pounding. He was turning away in despair when he saw her coming down the hall.

"Gib, Gib," she said, putting out both hands to keep him from crashing into her in his headlong rush. "What is it? What's wrong?"

"It's Georgie, Miss Mooney," Gib gasped. "Georgie Olson. He's back. He's in the office. I think he's dying."

Without waiting to ask any more questions, Miss Mooney turned and ran toward the stairs, Gib trailing behind her. At the office door she paused only long enough to knock once before she went right on in. Mr. Harding and Miss Offenbacher were standing near the desk, and Bobby, eyes bulging and chin quivering, was still propping up the sagging Georgie.

They all spoke at once.

Mr. Harding's furious "Where have you been, Whittaker? Who gave you permission to . . ." overlapped Miss Offenbacher's stern "You may leave, Miss Mooney. Mr. Harding and I can handle . . ."

Miss Mooney was speaking, too, but her soft, pleading "But—But Gibson says Georgie is very ill" wasn't nearly enough. Not enough to make them listen to her, Gib thought, and not nearly enough to make them let her help Georgie. But then, just as Gib was despairing all over again, Bobby came to the rescue by letting out a dismal wail, turning loose of Georgie, and collapsing in a useless lump of misery. Georgie, no longer supported, sank down sideways and slithered limply onto the floor. A moment later Miss Mooney was kneeling beside him, lifting his eyelids, feeling the pulse in his neck, and then beginning to unwrap his bandaged hands. And telling everyone what to do in a strong, forceful, entirely unfamiliar voice.

"Mr. Harding. Bring me a blanket and a hot-water bottle. Miss Offenbacher, please telephone the doctor immediately. And tell him to hurry."

To Gib's amazement, both Mr. Harding and Miss Offenbacher did what they were told. A few minutes later, as the three grown-ups clustered around Georgie's blanket-wrapped body, Gib grabbed the back of Bobby's coat, lifted him to his feet, and quietly dragged him backward through the door and out into the hall. Once outside the office Bobby immediately came to life and almost beat Gib up the two flights to Senior Hall.

Back in the dormitory Gib and Bobby quickly found themselves surrounded. Four or five boys at first, and then more as the seniors straggled back in from their chore assignments. It seemed that someone had seen them on their way to the office, and rumors and guesses had spread like wildfire.

Gib, and Bobby too, tried to answer their questions, but except for the stark, terrible fact that Georgie had run away and had been hiding, nearly frozen to death, in Juno's stall, the only news Gib and Bobby could give them was just what Georgie had told them before he passed out. That the man who had adopted him had punished him by sending him out without his mittens, and then had told Georgie the doctor was going to cut off his frozen hands.

But no one could answer the other questions. Questions like, what happened after Gib and Bobby left the office? Was Georgie alive or dead? Would they cut off his hands? Would he have to go back to live with Mr. Bean? And, over and over again, was it always that bad when you got adopted?

"Yeah," Thomas, a nine-year-old who had just come up from the juniors, said. "Remember when Georgie got adopted and we all thought he was so lucky?"

"Adopted," Jacob snorted. "Georgie wasn't adopted. He was farmed out."

Gib tried to shush him. After all, not only had they promised Buster they wouldn't tell who'd told them, they had also promised they wouldn't talk about it. "Shut up, Jacob." Gib poked him in the ribs. "Remember we said we wouldn't talk about it."

But Jacob ignored him, and before long the entire room was buzzing with talk about being farmed out and what it might be like for other senior boys who'd left in the last few months. Some of the younger boys just wouldn't believe that other adoptions, even ones that were obviously just farming outs, could be as bad as all that.

"We'd know about it, wouldn't we?" Abner asked. "Somebody would write and tell us."

"Who'd tell us?" Jacob said. "Old Offenbacher won't let us go to the library anymore, and they read our mail before we get to see it. Leastways that one letter I got from Herbie'd been read. And they probably throw it away if it says something they don't want us to know. And we only get to see the newspaper once in a while. Like when there's nothing in it that we're not supposed to see." Everyone was still staring at Jacob when Gib suddenly jumped to his feet, grabbed his coat off its peg, and started down the aisle.

"Where you going, Gib?" Jacob yelled.

At the door Gib turned back long enough to say, "To the barn. I got to go back to the barn. We forgot to feed Juno."

"Hey, come back," Jacob yelled. "You can't do that. It's suppertime."

"Yeah, I know." Gib was walking out the door backward. "I'll bet that's what Juno's thinking."

Jacob threw up his hands. "Okay. Go ahead. Get your dumb backside beaten to death. See if I care."

CHAPTER
13

That Friday night, the night they found Georgie in Juno's stall, seemed to go on and on forever. The blizzard finally blew itself out and a full moon shone down, making the whole outdoors into a coldly glittering world of snow and ice. Standing at a window in Senior Hall, his bare feet aching with the cold, Gib stared out into a cruel white world. And later, curled into a ball in his cot, he watched the brilliant moonlight make sliding patterns on the hardwood floors. Watched wide-eyed to keep from sleeping or even blinking, because the minute his eyes closed he was tormented by images that seemed to be printed on the insides of his eyelids.

Toward morning he slept a little, but every now and then he found himself wide awake, staring at the creeping patterns of moonlight and asking himself painful questions.

Questions about what had happened the day before,

and what might happen next. About Georgie mostly, and all the rest of the Lovell House boys who had been adopted or farmed out. And also about the ones who might be next to go.

Of course, there was no way to get any answers. No answers, and no hope of getting any for a long time. Not for hours, anyway, and maybe even days or weeks. Or quite likely not ever.

"We probably never will find out what they did with Georgie," Gib told Jacob as they were on their way down to breakfast the next morning. "It will probably be another secret that everybody guesses about but nobody knows the truth of."

Jacob agreed with him. "Yeah," he said. "Like that story about somebody dying in the Repentance Room a long time ago. Nobody knows if that's true."

Not long afterward, though, it began to look like there might be some news about Georgie after all. Breakfast was almost over when Miss Offenbacher came into the dining room and said she had an announcement to make. But the announcement only turned out to be that everyone above six years of age was to remain in the dining hall for a special assembly right after breakfast. The assembly, she said, would be about the rumors that were being spread around Lovell House that morning.

The assembly was about rumors all right, and not much else. Except for a brief mention that Georgie Olson was in the Harristown public hospital and was doing as well as could be expected, the whole assembly was about how destructive and evil the spreading of rumors could be, and how, as of that very day, the repetition of rumors would be severely punished. She didn't exactly come right out and say so, but what it came down to was that talking about Georgie Olson and what had happened to him was strictly forbidden.

Miss Mooney was at the assembly, too, along with all of the older juniors, but during Miss Offenbacher's talk she kept her eyes on her folded hands. Gib watched her a lot, hoping she would look up so he could catch her eye and make his face say how desperate he was to talk to her. But she didn't look up and the moment the assembly was over she slipped away. And from then on she went right on being slippery and silent, only shaking her head and hurrying off when anyone tried to ask questions.

In the days that followed there still were no answers about Georgie. No official answers, no Miss Mooney answers, and not even any discussions about Georgie, except in very small groups with a few trusted friends.

And the only other surprising thing that happened was that Gib never did get punished for the things he did that day, or for the things he didn't get done, either. No beating or Repentance Room time or even a scolding, though Juno hadn't been fed until very late, her stall never did get its Friday cleaning, and, on top of everything else, Gib had been late to supper.

Jacob said he couldn't figure that one out at all. "I mean, why did the old Paddleman let such a good excuse get away from him? Golly, Gib, he's whupped you for a lot less than that a whole lot of times."

"Yeah, I know," Gib said. "I can't figure it out. Unless . . ."

"Unless what?"

"I don't know. Unless it's that they just didn't want to do anything that would remind anyone about Georgie. So if I got beat on for trying to help Georgie, that was just going to remind everyone." He grinned and shrugged. "Or maybe Mr. Paddle just plain old gave up on saving me from hell. Maybe he just decided to let the old devil have me."

Jacob snorted. "Yeah, that must be it. You're a hopeless case, Whittaker, and that's for sure."

But unfortunately Mr. Paddle's loss of interest in Gib didn't last. In February he got whipped for losing his homework and a few weeks later for being late to supper again.

So by early spring Gibson Whittaker's life at Lovell House had fallen back into the same old pattern. Not any better and not much worse, except at night. In bed at night, waiting to go to sleep, or waking up in the deep, still quiet of early morning, his mind continued to skirt around the adopted family hope dream, but it wasn't the same anymore. Instead of the comfortingly boring story about other kids and animals and a mother who read books at bedtime, it had become a treacherous nightmare. A horror story that, starting out in the old way would, as daydream turned into dream, suddenly include a sour-faced, bearded man who stalked through a dimly lit room staring into one face and then another.

Or at other times the scene would fade into a dark, fear-haunted mist out of which a cringing, whimpering shadow would slowly emerge. A pitiful shadow whose bandaged arms reached out to Gib as if begging for help. And then Gib would be wide awake, looking up into the darkness and wishing desperately for morning to come.

Winter melted into spring, and spring had begun to green toward summer, when one morning at breakfast Buster came into the hall with a report notice for Gib. The notice said that Gibson Whittaker was to report to the headmistress's office at one o'clock.

"The office?" Bobby asked him. "What did you do now, Gib? And how come the office, I wonder, instead of Harding's torture chamber?"

"I don't know," Gib said. "I guess it'll be the Repentance Room, but I don't know why. What do you suppose I did this time?"

"I'll bet it's 'cause you laughed at the wrong time again," Jacob said. "When Offenbacher was reading the chore assignments and she almost said Bacob and Jobby. You know, when she said, 'Bacob and Job—er—Jacob and Bobby will be in the laundry.' "

Gib shook his head. "I didn't even smile," he said. "I'm pretty sure I didn't."

"You must have," Jacob insisted. "Anyway, I think you're mighty lucky getting sent to the Repentance

Room instead of to the laundry with Bobby and me." He grinned. "I mean, since ghosts and stuff like that don't bother you none, you can just repent a little and then curl up and have a nice long nap."

"Yeah," Bobby agreed. "While me and Jacob are breaking our backs and wearing the skin off our knuckles."

Gib grinned, too. "I'll be thinking about you and those old scrubbing boards while I'm having a good long nap up there in the Repentance Room."

He'd made that up to tease Jacob and Bobby, but on the way to the office he did try to tell himself that the Repentance Room really wouldn't be too bad on such a warm day. It was at least a slightly comforting thought, but Bobby and Jacob and the weather and everything else faded from his mind a moment later when he walked into Miss Offenbacher's office.

For a horrible moment Gib thought the man who was sitting in front of Miss Offenbacher's desk was the same one who had taken Georgie Olson. Like Mr. Bean, the man had gray hair and a lean, gray-bearded face. But after the shock of that first glance began to wear off, Gib could see that it wasn't the same man at all. This man's beard was shorter and more neatly trimmed, and his eyes were wider and not so deep-set.

When Gib began to come out of his terrified paralysis Miss Offenbacher was saying, "Here he is, Mr. Thornton. I take it this is the boy you had in mind?"

"Yes, yes," the man said, getting to his feet and motioning for Gib to approach. "I believe so." Putting his hand on Gib's shoulder, he asked, "What is your name, boy? And how old are you?"

"G-Gib," Gib stammered. "Gibson Whittaker, sir. Ten, sir. Eleven in December."

The man nodded slowly and then asked, "Where were you born?"

Gib was shaking his head when Miss Offenbacher interrupted. "We've made it a policy not to give full orphans any information of that sort. We've found that in some cases it only leads to attempts to—"

"I see," the man interrupted. "That's quite all right. I'm satisfied that this is the boy I'm looking for."

Releasing Gib's shoulder, he turned away, sat down at the desk, and as Gib's mind reeled with fear and dread, and then the faintest echo of old hopes, the gray-bearded man signed the papers that transferred to his care and guidance one Gibson Whittaker, ten-year-old ward of the state and resident of the Lovell House Home for Orphaned and Abandoned Boys.

CHAPTER

14

The buggy was large and well made and the high-stepping bays were sleek and fat. From his perch on the driver's seat next to the man called Mr. Thornton, Gib could look down across shiny bay backs and floating black tails and manes. Could almost lose himself in watching the beautiful team and forget about the stern-faced man who sat next to him saying nothing at all for mile after long, slow mile.

Nothing, that is, since Miss Offenbacher and Mr. Harding came out to see them off and to explain that no, there would be no luggage, since the orphanage policy was that any spare articles of clothing would be retained by the institution to be used by other residents. Looking surprised and a little bit annoyed, Mr. Thornton had only said, "I see," and, slapping the reins on the bays' backs, pulled away from Lovell House at a fast trot. It wasn't until they had reached the end of Lovell Avenue and turned off onto Fairfax Street that he began to ask questions. Not many questions and not as if they were a part of a conversation, but only now and then with maybe a half mile of silence in between.

"Well then, young man," he said suddenly as the bays trotted into the turn onto Willow Road and headed out across the prairie. Startled, Gib swallowed hard, found his voice, and said, "Yes sir?"

"You say you don't recall where you were born. What memories *do* you have of your life before your—before you arrived at Lovell House?"

"Not very much, sir. I think I remember my mother a little. And the horses we had—a bay and a sorrel mare—and a little bit about the house where I lived. And a wagon. I kind of recollect a buckboard wagon."

Mr. Thornton nodded. "Do you recall how old you were when your—when you came to Lovell House?"

"Six. I was six years old, sir. Miss Mooney, she's one of the teachers, she told me so."

Mr. Thornton nodded and went on driving in silence. Silence except for the creak and whir of the buggy and the steady *clop clop* of hooves. Those sounds, the beat of hooves and the grate of wheels on gravel, would, in the days and weeks to come, bring back over and over again the memory of that buggy ride. Would re-create in Gib's mind that strange journey to a new life, with its dream-like tangle of fear and dread shot through with brief moments of hopeful anticipation.

Gib kept trying to tell himself that in spite of every-thing, there really was some reason to hope. While Mr. Thornton didn't seem particularly warm and friendly, he didn't look to be cruel or violent, either. A quiet man, certainly, sitting there without a word for mile after long prairie mile, but perhaps a man who would answer a question or two if they were politely asked.

Lifting his eyes from the team, Gib stole a glance at the man seated beside him, a glance that told him that Mr. Thornton's suit was much more clean and sharp-looking than the bulky overcoat Mr. Bean had worn, or even than the suit Mr. Harding wore every day in his classroom. And while he didn't really believe that cleanli-ness was next to godliness, like Miss Mooney said, that snappy suit did seem encouraging. It was encouraging to think that a clean, neat, well-dressed man would not be at all like Mr. Bean, or even Mr. Harding. Gib was still checking out the gold cuff links and watch chain and the shiny leather of high-topped black shoes when Mr. Thornton turned and stared at him for a long time with-out smiling or saying a word.

Quickly shifting his gaze back to the smartly trotting horses, Gib decided that it would be best to wait to ask important questions. Questions whose answers would tell him where he would be living, and whether he'd be al-lowed to go to school, and if he'd be starved and sent out in freezing weather without any mittens. And that other question that he hardly dared even to think about—if he was being really adopted or only farmed out. Instead he would concentrate on the beautiful horses and shut his mind to those kinds of questions.

But there were other things as well that it didn't pay to think about, and one of them was that he had left Lovell House without telling anyone good-bye. Thinking about Miss Offenbacher's refusal to let him tell Jacob and Bobby, or even Miss Mooney, good-bye made a cramping pain in Gib's stomach.

He was still trying not to think about not ever seeing Jacob and Bobby again when Mr. Thornton began to talk, this time asking more questions about the orphanage. "I understand there was a change in the administration a while back," he said, and when Gib didn't respond, he added, "When Mrs. Hansen died?"

"Yes sir," Gib said emphatically, glad to have understood what Mr. Thornton was driving at. "A real big change. Everybody liked Mrs. Hansen." He thought for a moment before he added, "Miss Offenbacher was a big change all right." Then, realizing what he'd as good as said, he winced, wondering if he was in trouble. More questions about Lovell House followed, and Gib was trying hard to answer without saying things he shouldn't when the buggy topped a slight rise and he could see the outskirts of a town set along the edge of a wide river. Gib gasped in surprise, and Mr. Thornton pulled the buggy to a stop.

"Yes?" Mr. Thornton said, looking at Gib questioningly. "Longford. Do you remember Longford?"

"Longford," Gib whispered. "Longford." The name seemed to be attached to something far back in his mind, but when he reached for the spot it quickly faded. He was still reaching a few minutes later, trying to recall what that name had meant to him, when the bays picked up their pace eagerly as they approached a turnoff to a tree-lined drive. Mr. Thornton let them have their heads as they turned off the road, passing under a sign that said ROCKING M RANCH, followed by a capital *M* that sat on a curved line like the rocker on a chair: M

The house was beautiful. Not a great stone castle, like Lovell House, but a large and sturdy two-story home surrounded by wide porches and shaded by old trees. A solid, forever kind of place so much like the ones he'd pictured in his dreams of the future that for a moment the quick, warm thrill of hope was back again, singing in his ears and tightening his throat.

Gib was staring at the house when he thought he saw something in an upstairs window. He'd had only a quick glimpse, but he was almost sure that it had been a face. A pale, pointed face topped by something large and white, a hat maybe or a hair ribbon. He was still staring back over his shoulder when the team trotted through a yard surrounded by barns and sheds, turned into a narrow lane, turned again, and came to a stop in front of another house. A much smaller house this time, with unpainted walls and a steeply pitched roof of patchy shingles. Pulling the team to a stop, Mr. Thornton turned to look at Gib.

"You'll be staying here for now," he said, "with Hy?" A testing question seemed to be there again, but when Gib didn't respond he added, "Hyram Carter?" Another testing, but Gib could only shake his head. Mr. Thornton shrugged and went on, "Hy was the foreman on the Rocking M and now—"

At that moment hinges creaked loudly as the cabin door swung open and crashed back against the wall, sending the team into a series of skittish sidesteps. Gib was watching the team's shenanigans when he heard a voice say, "Sorry about that, boss. Durned crutch got away from me. Almost took a header." The raspy, rough-edged voice produced a faint echo in Gib's head, an echo that seemed to come from far back among the deepest shadows.

The man standing in the cabin door was long and lean with a wild mop of wiry gray hair and a dark, sunscorched face. He was wearing a denim shirt, a worn leather vest, and a pair of baggy denim stockpants—with only one leg. Stockpants with the left leg cut off above a heavy cast that extended from just above the knee down to his ankle. Hopping forward, he was bending down to retrieve his crutch when Gib suddenly came out of a trance of crowding shadows, saw what needed to be done, and jumped down from the buggy. Picking up the crutch, he handed it to the weather-beaten man, stared into his face, and knew with a rush of wild, warm excitement that he had known him before. Somewhere, sometime, he had known this man before.

"Well, well, well." Hy was steadying himself with one hand on Gib's shoulder as he maneuvered the crutch around to his left side. "If it isn't the little Whittaker dogie come back to the home range. Ol' Gibby Whittaker nigh onto being growed up, sure as God made little apples."

CHAPTER

15

So the man named Hyram Carter *was* someone he'd known before. Gib was reaching back, concentrating so hard on trying to remember who and when, that he was only vaguely aware of the conversation between Hy and Mr. Thornton.

"No, very little," Mr. Thornton was saying when Gib began to listen. "He seems to remember almost nothing. Strange, really."

"Not so strange, considerin' what he'd just gone through." Shifting on his crutches, the man called Hy went on, "But he's Gibby Whittaker all right. No doubt about that. And he knew me right off, didn't you, boy?"

Gib gasped, grinned uncertainly, and nodded. "I think so, sir. I think I used to know you, but I don't know who you are. I feel all . . ." He glanced up at Mr. Thornton. "My head feels—mixed up."

Hy's smile widened. "Well, don't you go worryin' none

about that. Just tell the boss thanks for drivin' all the way to Harristown to fetch you, and then come on in."

Gib did as he was told. "Yes—yes sir," he said. "Thanks for fetching . . ." But Mr. Thornton was already turning the team, and a minute later Gib was inside the cabin, the clop and jingle of the buggy fading as it went back down the lane.

The cabin was very small. One room with a table, two chairs, a rusty iron range at one end, and a bunk bed built into the wall at the other. Near the bed a ladder led up to a loft. Hy was standing near the table, his eyes fixed on Gib and a strange half smile on his dark, wrinkle-puckered face, when a sudden, crazy idea exploded in Gib's head. Before he could stop it, it came out of his mouth. "Are you—my father?"

Hy's laugh had a harsh honking sound to it, like the horn of a motorcar. He honked until he almost choked himself—coughed alarmingly, slapped his chest—and honked some more. "Naw!" he said when he'd finally stopped laughing. " 'Fraid not, pardner. But I knew your papa once upon a time, and your mama too."

"You knew . . ." Gib swallowed hard and swallowed again. For a moment his mind refused to take it in—or believe that it was true. That he had found the place where he belonged, or at least where the people he belonged to had once lived. It was a while before he managed to say, "Where—I mean—when . . . ?"

The man called Hy propped his crutches against the table, lowered himself into a chair, and said, "Well now,

if you'd pour us some java—pot's there on the range—
and sit yourself down here, I'll tell you a thing or two."
He rolled his eyes toward the fading sound of the buggy
and, grinning in a way that seemed to hint at hidden
meanings, he added, "Leastways all the law allows."

Coffee had never been included in the Lovell House
diet, and as Gib poured the second cup he eyed the dark,
grainy liquid with some misgivings. But he did as he was
told, and a moment later he was sitting across the table
from the man who had known his parents, who knew
who he was and where he had come from. He clutched
the cup of coffee with both shaky hands and watched as a
whirlpool of thoughts and feelings seemed to repeat itself
in the swirling liquid.

Hy sipped his coffee, cleared his throat, and stared
squinty-eyed, not at Gib himself but at something faint
and far away that he seemed to be trying to bring into
focus.

"Must have met your folks sometime in the late nine-
ties, not long after they came to Longford. Up from
Kansas, I think they were. Bought the old Anders place.
Nice little spread just south of the Rocking M land. A
mite small for ranchin', but not too bad neither. Seems as
how your ma had been a teacher back in Kansas and she
taught here in Longford for a year or so. Up until you
came along. But then, when you weren't much more than
a toddler, your pa . . ." Hy paused, looking at Gib
closely. "Your pa got himself killed in a huntin' accident."

"Nineteen one," Gib said, triumphant that he knew

and remembered something, anything at all, about his past. "Miss Mooney said it was in the records. That my father died in nineteen one."

Hy nodded. "Sounds about right." He sighed. "Your ma did her best to keep things goin'. Hired extra help when she had to, and did an awful lot of the work her own self. A lot more'n a pint-sized little lady like her ought to have had to do. Folks from the church did what they could to help, and I helped out now and then with the stock." His eyes shifted and refocused on Gib. "That's why you're rememberin' 'bout me, more'n likely. Saw a lot of me in those days. Used to follow me around like a pup dog, watchin' and asking all kinds of questions." Hy chuckled. "Questions about handlin' stock, mostly, specially horseflesh. Never saw a kid so plum crazy about horses. I taught you how to sneak a bit 'twixt a pony's teeth myself, and after that you used to ride your ma's gentle old bay Morgan ever chance you got. When you warn't more'n four, five year old you'd climb up on a fence with your pockets full of oats and the bridle 'round your neck, and when that old bay—"

"Amos," Gib interrupted excitedly. "His name was Amos."

"Right you are. Amos it was. You'd have a bridle on him and be across his neck quick as lightning and sliding on down it to his withers." Hy laughed. "And once you got there you stuck like a burr."

The bay's name *was* Amos, Gib thought delightedly. Delighted that he was remembering and that he did have something to remember after all. He really had come from someplace and had his own people, and horses too that had belonged to him. Horses that were a part of who he was and where he came from. After all those years of not knowing, of wishing and wondering, it was a wonderfully exciting and satisfying thing to consider.

Suddenly Hy's grin disappeared and the laughter gullies that creased his cheeks shifted solemnly downward. "You remember your ma, don't you? She was one fine lady."

Gib wanted to say he remembered everything about her. Not just her name on the records, and a few faint memories about what she did to an old horse beater, and some dreamlike scenes from the books she read at bedtime. "I remember her name was Maggie," he said, "and—and she read a lot." He paused, then went on reluctantly, "But I don't know what happened to her. I never knew what happened to her."

Hy put down his coffee and stared at Gib. Then, speaking slowly and solemnly, he said, "She died, boy, in the epidemic of 1904. Lots of folks sickened that year all over the territory. Bad water, it was. At least that's what was said later. At the time nobody knew what caused it. You took sick first, real bad sick. And then when your ma came down with it you was took to a clinic they'd set up down by the old church. Folks there took real good care of you, I guess, but . . ." Hy sighed deeply and went back to staring off into the past. He was still staring when someone knocked on the cabin door. An alarming

100

knock that had a loud firmness to it, almost a headmistress kind of sound. Gib looked anxiously at Hy, who seemed puzzled for a moment before he nodded and grinned.

"You get the latch, Gibby," he said. "Wouldn't be surprised if it's for you anyways. Leastways in a manner of speakin'."

Maybe Hy wasn't surprised, but Gib certainly was. When the door swung wide open the person standing there was not Mr. Thornton or anyone else he'd ever seen before. Except maybe just a glimpse in an upstairs window. The person standing in the cabin door was small; she was dressed in lots of pale yellow ruffles, and there was a big white ribbon on top of her head.

Gib was regarding her in openmouthed surprise when the girl cocked her head, narrowed her blue eyes, and said to Hy, "He looks just about like I thought he would." She nodded thoughtfully. " 'Cept maybe taller and not so . . ." She paused, looked Gib over from head to toe, and then shrugged. Walking clear around him and back to Hy, she said, "I came to tell you that we're all eating in the kitchen at five-thirty. All right?" She turned then, and on her way back out the door she stared at Gib again.

When she had gone and Gib had relatched the door, Hy broke into his honking laugh. "What's so funny?" Gib asked warily.

"Supper's always at five-thirty," Hy chortled. "Leastways when it's in the kitchen. Oh, once in a blue moon when there's important company the boss and the missus eat real late in the dinin' room, but mostly it's just in the kitchen with the hired help. At five-thirty on the nose."

Gib frowned thoughtfully. "Then why . . . ?"

"Not hard to figure," Hy said. "Miss Livy just come to get a look at you. She's been nigh onto dyin' of curiosity for the last week or two, ever since . . ." He paused. "Well, ever since her folks decided to . . ." He paused again, narrowed his eyes, and then went on, "Decided to look you up."

"Look me up?" Gib repeated, but then Hy slapped his hand down on the table and began to struggle to his feet.

"Here we sit gabbin' when we got enough work to keep the both of us busy right up till dinnertime. Come on, pardner," Hy said, reaching for his crutches. "Help me prop myself up on these old peg legs, and I'll start showin' you the ropes."

CHAPTER
16

The Thorntons' barn was as solidly built as the house itself, and a lot bigger. A shiny buggy, the one Gib had ridden in with Mr. Thornton, sat in the central corridor, and on each side were box stalls. A great many box stalls, ten or more on each side. The barn smelled wonderfully of oats and hay and sweated leather and the sharp, warm, exciting smell of horses.

Caesar and Comet, the bay team that Gib had met before, were in the first two stalls, and on the right side across the corridor a blue roan stuck his head out over the half door and nickered coaxingly. And suddenly the quiver was there again in the farthest corners of Gib's mind, the deeply buried stirring of something almost remembered.

"All right, you old beggar," Hy was saying. "Be right with you. Got ourselves a new wrangler here who's going to be looking out for you." Turning to Gib, he said,

103

"Roan's mine. Had him nigh onto twenty years now, since he was just a yearlin'. Best cutting horse I—"

"Lightning," Gib interrupted excitedly. "Lightning?" He made it into a question, and Hy nodded, grinning.

"Right again," he said. "Old Blue Lightnin'." One eyebrow crept up. "So you remember Lightnin'."

Gib's nod was enthusiastic—exultant. "I do. I do now. I wouldn't have if somebody just asked me, maybe, but seeing him, seeing the way his mane flops over like that, and how his forehead kind of tucks down over his eyes, it—it just came back like. All of a sudden I saw him trotting down a road, stepping high and tossing his head."

"Sounds like my old blue devil all right," Hy said, rubbing the quivering nose. "Always did have a full head of steam in him."

It was then, peeking over the next door, that Gib saw something that almost took his breath away. The mare in the next stall was a thing to look at, long-legged and high-necked, solid black except for a white blaze on her forehead and three white feet. A little jumpy, though, Gib thought as she eyed him curiously from across the stall, flicking her ears back and forth. Gib was still hanging over the door when Hy swung up beside him on his crutches.

"Got to watch this one," Hy said. "Not mean. No sirree. Not mean at all." Hy shook his head firmly, as if someone were arguing with him. "Just high-spirited and a mite skittish."

"She yours too?" Gib asked, gazing in awe at the elegant creature, but Hy only shook his head.

"Silky? No. 'Fraid not. Black Silk here's from bluegrass country. The missus got all sorts of fancy papers on her. Used to be her pleasure-ridin' horse. 'Fraid nobody rides her much now." They both stood quietly as the mare approached cautiously, snorting and showing the whites of her eyes. Gib was holding out his hand when Hy clapped him on the back.

"That's all there is now, 'cept for the mules, down t'other end. All those fancy box stalls just goin' to waste." He shrugged. "Come on now, let's get to it. Lots to do. I'll show you the ropes and then I'll brush down the boss's team a bit while you take care of the feedin'."

Gib's job, at least the first part, which consisted of climbing the ladder to the loft and sending down a double flake of hay to each of the four horses and two mules, was easy and fun. And rationing out the oats was even better. He really liked going into each stall, being nickered at and nudged by velvety noses as he poured out the oats. Into each of the stalls, that is, except the black mare's.

Hy insisted on feeding Black Silk. Balancing on one crutch and holding the oat can with the other hand, he made his way into the stall and out again while the mare stood back and eyed the crutch suspiciously, flicking her ears and rolling her eyes.

"Maybe you can take over tomorrow or the next day,"

Hy told Gib, "after she's had a bit of a chance to get used to you."

There were other chores after the horses: feeding and watering the chickens, gathering eggs, and feeding the cow. And soon, Hy said, there would be some gardening, and the milking too. According to Hy, Mrs. Perry, who was the Thorntons' cook and housekeeper, had been doing the milking lately but wasn't happy about it. So that was to be a part of Gib's job too, as soon as he got the hang of it. And when Gib said he already knew how to milk because he'd learned at the orphanage, Hy looked surprised and said as how Mrs. Perry was going to be mighty pleased to hear that they taught the orphans at that awful place something useful.

The last chore was delivering the eggs to the cooler on the porch of the big house, and then came washing up at a long metal trough near the kitchen door. By then it was time for supper. The five-thirty meal that the girl named Livy had come all the way down the lane to Hy's cabin to announce.

As he was hanging up the towel Hy said, " 'Bout having meals with the boss's family. It's kind of a leftover from the days when this place used to be the home spread for the Rocking M Ranch. Merrill family owned the Rocking M back then, and the missus used to be Julia Merrill 'fore she married Mr. Thornton. Grew up right here on the ranch, she did. Back in those days all the hired hands used to eat in the kitchen with the family."

Hy's grin had a hazy, remembering look to it. "A dozen people, closer to twenty during roundups," he went on. "Used to get pretty lively sometimes back then, but . . ." He paused. "Things are different now. Different," he said again, Gib could tell that the difference was somehow important.

"Different?" he asked.

"Yeah," Hy said. "Well, quieter like. Bein' a banker and all, Mr. Thornton likes things to be sort of polite and quiet like." He grinned. "Quiet, 'specially."

Gib had a feeling Hy was trying to tell him something without really saying it.

"Quiet," he repeated, nodding, and Hy grinned and nodded back.

Gib told himself he wouldn't forget.

The kitchen in the big house was pretty amazing. Amazingly huge and warm and good-smelling. It was an enormous room with a long rectangular table running down the center and, around the walls, cupboards, sinks, worktables, and two big cooking ranges. At one end of the long table there were place settings for—five, six, seven, Gib counted—seven people. Yes, he thought, a large family.

Looking around the room, breathing in the mouthwatering smells, and then counting the seven place settings, Gib felt an unexpected rush of hope. A fleeting feeling that here it was, a scene right out of his dream. But then the people began to arrive, and they were not one big family and not at all like the people he had always imagined.

A woman came in first. A large roundish woman with a face to match who was wearing a gingham dress and apron and carrying a big pitcher. When she saw Gib she stopped, stared, and then said, "Well, glory be. So this is finally the boy from the orphanage." Setting the pitcher down on the table, she put her hands on her hips and went on staring, nodding her large, round head.

Gib was wondering if . . . and then deciding that no, this couldn't be the Mrs. Thornton who had ridden the mare named Black Silk, when three more people came in. Two more women and then Mr. Thornton himself, still dressed in a dark suit and high-collared shirt.

The two women were very different-looking. The older one was tall and thin with a narrow, bony face, a plain, dark dress, and lots of wiry gray hair. The other was probably the most elegant woman Gib had ever seen. She was wearing a dress made of a deep blue shiny material, there was lace around her wrists and neck, and a great pile of brown hair was arranged in sleek coils on top of her small head. She looked, Gib decided, as elegant as the black mare and almost as beautiful. But the beautiful woman didn't walk into the room like the others. Sitting in a thronelike chair, she was pushed through the door and up to the table by the woman with the thin face and sharp, quick eyes.

Gib had never seen a wheelchair before, but he'd heard about them. He was still staring when the beautiful woman turned, looked directly at him, and said, "Well, hello there, Gibson Whittaker. So here you are at last."

Just then there was the sound of running feet. The door flew open, and the girl who had visited Hy's cabin shot into the room, skidded to a stop, and then, ignoring Gib completely, walked primly to the end of the table and sat down next to the woman in the wheelchair. And when the woman said, "Livy dear, this is Gibson Whittaker," she only glanced at him briefly and turned away. "I know," she said coolly. "The boy from the orphanage."

CHAPTER

17

Late that night, as he tossed restlessly on a squeaky cot in the loft of Hy's cabin, Gib's mind spun with a bewildering confusion of vivid mental pictures, unanswered questions, and up-and-down emotions.

The pictures came first. Most often and most shocking, a picture of Mr. Thornton in his long, dark coat seated in front of Miss Offenbacher's desk. That scene flashed up again and again, and with it always came the same quick flicker of nightmare terror as when, at first glimpse, the man had looked so much like Georgie's Mr. Bean.

Other images stirred up other feelings. The feeling of hope when he had first seen the Thorntons' big, old tree-sheltered house. And the bewildered excitement that had flared when Hy stumbled out of the cabin. Dusty old Hy with his tumbleweed hair, broken leg, and leathery face. A face that had caused one of those vibrations that promised, but didn't always produce, a buried memory. But with Hy the memory had burst free, and Gib had known for sure and certain that he had not only seen this man before but also heard that creaky voice and strange honking laugh.

Other pictures . . . the huge old barn with its four horses. Its four beautiful horses. Thinking about the horses, Gib shivered even though the night was warm and there were plenty of blankets on the squeaky cot.

And then there was the mouthwatering image of the Thorntons' kitchen with its long table loaded down with wonderful food. Oven-roasted meat and fresh vegetables and freshly baked bread. And peach pie for dessert. Never in his life had Gib eaten anything so delicious as that thick slab of peach pie. Full as he was now, he still enjoyed reliving the eating, tasting all of it over and over again in his imagination and comparing it to the grainy soups or mushy stews that, along with a slice of bread, were all there was to a Lovell House supper.

The kitchen scene went on and on, around the table and back again. Mr. Thornton first, gray-bearded, dark-suited Mr. Thornton, who sat at the head of the table and read a paper and spoke very little. And then the beautiful lady in the thronelike wheelchair, who, just as Gib had guessed, was Mrs. Thornton.

Mrs. Julia Thornton, who had grown up here on the Thornton land when it was the Rocking M Ranch, and who had owned and ridden the black mare. And who smiled at Gib every time she noticed him staring.

During the meal Mrs. Thornton and the other women, Mrs. Perry, the cook, and the tall gray one, whose name was Miss Hooper, had done almost all of the talking. Quiet talk, mostly about things like a church supper that was being planned and a new batch of baby chicks that had hatched that morning.

There were vivid mind pictures, too, of the girl called Livy—or sometimes Olivia. Seen at the other end of the table, without the element of shocked surprise that had accompanied her sudden appearance at the cabin door, she had at first seemed rather elegant, too. Or interesting, anyway. Interestingly unlike anything Gib had ever imagined in his daydream families. The girls he had pictured had tended to be vaguely shy and pale, not at all like this head-tossing, high-spirited person with her frowning dark blue eyes.

During dinner Gib had watched her cautiously from time to time, but whenever she saw him looking she frowned and tossed her head in a way that jiggled her big white hair ribbon and the thick mass of brown curls that hung down her back. She didn't say anything to him, though. Most of the time she didn't say anything to anyone, but now and then she talked to the women, particularly when they were discussing the baby chicks.

"I helped one of them hatch," she'd said. "Its shell had a sticky skin inside it that wouldn't break and the chick couldn't get out so I peeled a little of it off and it came out all wet and sticky and—" She broke off suddenly, looking at her father, who was frowning at her over the top of his paper.

"Olivia," he said sharply, and then, turning to the gray-haired woman, he went on, "Miss Hooper, don't you agree that discussions of such barnyard procedures are hardly appropriate during a meal? Perhaps a lesson on suitable dinnertime conversation would be in order."

"Yes," Miss Hooper said, "I quite agree. Olivia and I will discuss it when the opportunity arises."

Watching the girl right then, Gib had noticed how a muscle in her cheek tightened and twitched angrily. And when she caught Gib looking, her glare was fiercer than ever. Gib couldn't help wondering what he'd done to make her so angry.

At their end of the table Hy said nothing at all unless he was spoken to, and neither did Gib. Remembering Hy's warning, Gib had been careful to be very quiet.

Outside the cabin the wind increased, hissing around corners and rattling loose shingles, so that even after the pictures faded Gib couldn't fall asleep. It was then that the questions began. Hy had answered some of them, but now it seemed that there were even more that had been left unanswered. Questions about exactly where his home had been and what it had been like, and why his memories had always been so vague and confused. There was so much more that he wanted to know.

Then there was another question that hadn't occurred

to him at first but that now seemed to be terribly important. Why had Mr. Thornton come for him? If the Thorntons had known him all those years ago, and had known he was at Lovell House, why hadn't they come to get him before? Why did they wait until . . . But then, suddenly, Gib thought he knew at least that one answer. Buster had given him the answer when he had explained how nobody wanted to farm out a boy who was too young to be useful.

Gib sighed. So that was it, then. He had definitely been farmed out, just like Georgie and Herbie. He was here at the Thorntons' as what Buster had called slave labor, an unpaid milker of cows and gatherer of eggs and cleaner of stalls and who knew what else.

Rolling over on the squeaky cot, Gib rewrapped himself in blankets and tried, just as he'd always tried at Lovell House, to concentrate on hopeful thoughts. Like the food, for instance. Unless this evening had been a special occasion, which nobody had said it was, it certainly didn't look like he was going to starve to death, at any rate.

And then there was that other, even more comforting, thought. The one about how Hy had called him the new wrangler. A wrangler was the cowboy who was in charge of the horses on roundup. Rolling over again, Gib wrapped himself in the thought of being a wrangler, and before long went to sleep.

CHAPTER

18

Gib went to sleep that first night at the Thorntons' dreaming about horses, but he woke up the next morning wondering about school. It was a school day, and if he had still been at Lovell House he would soon have been in the seniors' classroom studying history and the parts of speech—and trying to keep from smiling when Jacob made faces behind Mr. Harding's back.

It was surely a school day in Longford too, although nothing had been said about whether Gib would be attending. Perhaps he wouldn't be going to school at all? He smiled, thinking what Jacob would say about some people having all the luck. But Buster hadn't been feeling that way when he said that some farmed-out kids didn't get to go to school at all.

Gib was planning to ask Hy about school, but he hadn't yet mentioned it when the subject came up without his asking. It happened as they were on their way to the cow barn in the pale half-light of early dawn, on what was looking to be the start of an extra-warm spring day.

"Gotta shake a leg," Hy was saying. "Way the boss has things laid out, we gotta get the feedin' and milkin' done afore breakfast time, and the bays hitched up to the buggy too. Elsewise Miss Livy'll be late for school agin."

Gib's opinion of Livy and small girls in general went up a notch. "Livy drives the bays to school?" he asked, surprised and impressed.

Hy chuckled. "Naw. I guess she'd like to well enough, but she rides into town with her pa when he goes in to the bank, 'cept when the weather's real bad. But she's the one who has to hurry. Guess schoolmarms like to get things goin' a mite earlier than bankers do. From what I hear tell, the boss drives her to school and then goes to the downtown cafe and has himself a second cup of java afore he opens up the bank."

"And what happens when the weather's real bad?" Gib asked.

"Why, then Miss Livy stays home and her mother and Miss Hooper take care of her schoolin'." Hy turned to look at Gib questioningly. "What you asking about schoolin' for?" He grinned. "You itchin' to get back to school already?"

"Well . . ." Gib hesitated, thinking about all the things Miss Mooney had said about the importance of learning. "Well, I was just wondering. . . ."

Hy chuckled. "Don't remember as how anybody discussed your eddication afore they decided to take you on. Leastways not in my hearin'. But maybe you can ask the missus 'bout it today. She wants to see you this morning when your chores are all done."

Gib found it disturbing that Mrs. Thornton wished to see him. He wanted to know more. He wanted to ask where and why, but they were in the cow barn by then and Hy was busy with advice and instruction. But as Gib put the silage in the feed pan, let Belle, the spotted cow, into the milking room, fastened the stanchion bar around her neck, and proceeded to demonstrate his skill as a milker, he went on wondering why Mrs. Thornton had asked to see him.

It wasn't until the milking was done and the fresh milk delivered to the cooler on the back veranda, the chickens and horses fed, and the bays hitched to the buggy that Hy said it was time to head on in for breakfast. Gib was standing at the stall door at the time, watching the black mare. This time Hy had let him take her oats into the stall, and while she hadn't wanted him to touch her, she had stood quietly enough, watching him with her ears pointed forward instead of flicking back and forth. As she ate she raised her head two times to look at him and quivered her nostrils in a way that was halfway between a snort and a nicker. Gib chuckled, thinking how she looked to be deciding that he wasn't such a dangerous hombre after all. But then Hy said again that it was time to get going, and Gib told the mare good-bye and tore himself away.

Breakfast that morning was pancakes and applesauce and fried eggs. Gib couldn't help smiling when he remembered Lovell House's gooey oatmeal, with a few raisins on special occasions, and how he and Jacob used to count the raisins and bet on who was going to get the most. He grinned, looked up to see Livy staring at him, and grinned at her too.

Livy Thornton was wearing another fancy dress. Red plaid this time, with a low waist and a big square collar. When Gib smiled at her, she frowned, looked away, pushed back her chair, and got up from the table.

Picking up a coat and a stack of books, she said, "I'll be in the buggy, Father," and went out the door. Mr. Thornton was still eating, and except for Hy and Mrs. Perry, who was busy at the stove, no one else was in the room.

When Mr. Thornton left a few minutes later, with only a brief nod in the direction of Hy and Gib, no one else had shown up. Not even Mrs. Thornton, who, according to Hy, wanted to talk to Gib today.

Hy was pushing back his chair. "Mighty fine flapjacks, Delia," he said. Hobbling over to where the cook was pouring a new batch of batter onto the griddle, he went on, "Can't understand for the life of me how the menfolk around here can let a fine-lookin', fine-cookin' lady like you stay a widow. I'd pop the question myself if I was the marryin'—"

Whirling around, Mrs. Perry said, "Get out of here,

you scallywag," and swatted at Hy with the pancake turner.

Hy limped away, pretending to be scared to death. Gib couldn't help laughing, and when Hy looked back at him and wiggled his eyebrows, Gib laughed even harder. And went on laughing even after Hy stopped clowning and headed for the door. And then went on laughing even after Hy turned around and gave him a puzzled frown.

Afterward Gib wondered why he'd laughed so hard. Because, after all, what Hy had done hadn't been all that funny. He couldn't figure it out, really, except that maybe it was just a sudden relief that the worst had happened—he'd been farmed out just like Herbie and Georgie—and he was still able to laugh. And right out loud, too.

He was following Hy out the door when he remembered about seeing Mrs. Thornton. Grabbing Hy's arm, he whispered, "The missus. When did she want to see me?"

"Later," Hy said. "Said she wanted to see you when your morning chores were done."

Gib almost said he thought he'd finished them, but it soon became obvious that he was a long way from it. He wouldn't be finished, it seemed, until he'd staked Belle out in the orchard, watered and hoed in the vegetable garden, and started in on cleaning out the box stalls, all of which looked to be in real bad shape.

Hy hung around most of the morning, leaning on his crutches, showing Gib where things were and commenting on how he was doing. And now and then reminding Gib that it had been the boss, Mr. Thornton himself, who had made up the list of chores that Gib was supposed to get done that day.

The garden was hard work, particularly the hoeing. Weeds had grown up in all the rows, and the hoe was old and not very sharp. Gib had done some hoeing in the orphanage garden that spring, but not a great deal, and his hands hadn't yet developed their summertime calluses. And then, with his hands already blistering from the hoe handle, there was the stall cleaning to look forward to, which would mean a lot of shovel work. Gib was starting on the second stall when Hy decided to go back to the cabin.

"You get that one finished and then wash up and go on in to see the missus," he said. "You can do Lightnin's later, and I'll come out to help with Silky's. I got to get off my feet for a spell."

The sun was high in the sky when Gib went back to the big house and washed up on the veranda, wincing when the soap made the blisters on his palms smart. Some of them had broken and dirt had worked its way in under the loose skin. He washed as best he could, took a deep breath, squared his shoulders, and went into the kitchen.

Miss Hooper and Mrs. Perry were seated at the kitchen table talking and drinking coffee. They stopped talking when Gib came in.

"Oh yes." Miss Hooper's voice, like the rest of her, was thin and sharp. "Mrs. Thornton said for you to go right on in." Getting up from the table, she led the way to a door, opened it, gestured, and then, as Gib passed her, she sniffed and said, "You're smelling a bit ripe, boy. Did you wash up? Here, let me see your hands." Taking his hands in hers, she inspected them carefully, squinting her pale eyes and frowning when she saw the palms.

"They're not dirty," Gib said hastily. "I washed just before I came in. Those are just blisters."

Miss Hooper nodded. "Just blisters," she said, nodding sharply. "So they are. Just blisters, indeed." Then she led Gib down the hall, knocked once on a door, and went in.

The large room was lined with bookshelves. Gib had never seen so many books in one place, except back in Mrs. Hansen's time, when a good reader could win an occasional trip to the Harristown Library. Across the room Mrs. Thornton was seated at a large desk in her high-backed wheelchair.

"Look at his hands, Julia," Miss Hooper said, and then went out, closing the door behind her with what was clearly a slam. Without meaning to, Gib put his hands behind his back.

The beautiful woman in the wheelchair smiled and motioned for him to come closer. "Your hands?" It was a question. And then when Gib reluctantly held them out, "Oh dear. How did you do that?"

"It was the shoveling and the hoeing, I guess," Gib

said. "They'll toughen up. They have before. I just haven't been doing as much shoveling lately and . . ."

Mrs. Thornton turned back to the desk and rang a bell. "I'm sure they will toughen up," she said. "But in the meantime I think we'd better get them a little cleaner."

The next half hour was spent doctoring Gib's hands. Miss Hooper, whom Julia called Hoop, came back and was sent out for a medicine kit and then was sent out again looking for gloves. "Look in my cedar chest," Mrs. Thornton said. "My old riding gloves will have to do until we can get some heavy work gloves that are small enough to fit him. And while you're at it, bring a measuring tape. Henry says he hasn't any other clothes, and he can't go on wearing these awful things."

Gib looked down at his Lovell House uniform of bulky dark blue serge. Of course the material never had been the best, and perhaps it had thinned out a little on the knees and elbows. And right at the moment the pants particularly were maybe a bit barnyardy. But he hadn't thought they were all that bad.

After a while he began to realize that while all the fuss over the blisters and clothing was embarrassing, it was turning out to feel kind of good, too. Good in the way it had felt when, once in a great while, he'd managed to get Miss Mooney's full attention. But it wasn't until his hands were doctored and bandaged and all his measurements taken that he began to find out why he'd really been sent for.

CHAPTER
19

"About Lovell House," Mrs. Thornton said when Miss Hooper finally disappeared, taking the medicine chest and tape measure with her. "Let's see. You must have been there since you were five or six years old?"

"Six," Gib agreed. He was sitting in a big armchair with his arms and hands resting on the fat plush-covered arms. He didn't like looking at his bandaged hands because, even though the bandages were much smaller and cleaner, they reminded him of . . . So he looked away—and noticed a shiny new telephone on Mrs. Thornton's desk, and then a glass bowl of hard candy.

"So you were in the orphanage for almost five years," Mrs. Thornton was saying. Then she handed Gib the bowl he'd been noticing and said, "Please have a peppermint. And then tell me all about Lovell House."

Gib hadn't meant to stare at the candy, but he'd had a

peppermint just last Christmas and he couldn't quite keep his mouth from watering as he remembered the taste. So he quickly said thanks, put a big round candy ball in his mouth, and began to talk around it. "It's a great big old building," he said, trying to keep the peppermint from rattling against his teeth. "Made of stone, and with a tower at each end, like a castle."

"Yes, I remember seeing it some years ago. But what was it like living there, Gib?"

He thought a minute. "Like?" he said. "Well . . ." He found it hard to go on in words that would mean anything to someone who'd never lived there. Who'd never lived in Junior Hall with dozens of other kids and not nearly enough of a lot of things to go around. And not nearly enough people like Miss Mooney to go around, either.

So he started by saying, "Well—I was a junior at first," and then hurried on to tell about how you were either an infant or junior or senior, depending on your age. Once he got that explained, it got easier, and he went on, telling about Miss Mooney, the housemother, and old Mrs. Hansen, who had been the headmistress for so many years. When he got to the part about Miss Offenbacher, he tried not to say too much about how she'd changed things, which wasn't easy because Mrs. Thornton seemed especially interested in the changes.

Now and then Gib tried to steer the conversation back to what had happened before Lovell House. "Hy says my folks lived near here. Did you know my mother?" he managed to ask once, and when Mrs. Thornton began to answer he felt a shiver of anticipation crawl up the back of his neck.

"Yes, I did." Mrs. Thornton paused and smiled. "She was a wonderful woman. Strong and brave and . . . and wonderful with horses."

Gib sat up straighter and almost choked on what was left of the peppermint. Mrs. Thornton was looking away—far away—as if remembering. Gib was getting ready to ask something he couldn't quite find the words for when Mrs. Thornton went on. "You've seen my Black Silk?"

"Yes. Yes, I have. She's beautiful."

"Yes, she is, isn't she." Mrs. Thornton smiled thoughtfully. "Your mother rode her once."

"My mother . . ." Gib's voice had gone strange on him, high and wobbly. "How did . . . how come . . ."

"It was a long time ago. Hy had started training Silk, but she was still pretty unpredictable. Your mother had come to see my husband about some banking business, I believe. But she saw me on Silk. No one had ridden the mare except me, and Hy of course, but I could see how well she reacted to Maggie—your mother, that is. So I loaned her a divided skirt and let her take Silk around the ring a few times." Mrs. Thornton's eyes were dreamy again. "Silk went amazingly well for her. Settled and quiet. Hy said that was what Silk needed. That kind of quieting skill."

Picturing a woman, a woman as beautiful as Mrs.

125

Thornton but with light-colored wispy hair, riding on the black mare made Gib feel almost paralyzed with excitement. "What did she—" he was beginning to say when a loud jangling noise that came from someplace nearby made him gasp and jump.

It was only the telephone. Although Gib had read about telephones and had seen the one on the headmistress's desk at Lovell House, he had never before heard one ring. Nor had he ever heard anyone talk on one. He watched, fascinated, as Mrs. Thornton rolled her chair nearer to the desk, lifted the hearing horn down from its hook, put it to her ear, and spoke into the cup-shaped mouthpiece.

"Yes . . . Yes, of course, Ellie," she said. "Put him on." Then she said, "Hello, Henry." After that she listened for quite a while saying only "yes" and "I know" now and then, but with her face changing slowly, going from warm and smiling to something quite different. Her voice had changed too when she finally said, "All right . . . All right. You're right. I did promise." Then she said "Good-bye" and hung the earpiece back on its hook.

Gib had tried not to listen, both because he felt he shouldn't and because what he was hearing, and sensing, made him uncomfortable. But even while he was trying not to listen he didn't forget what they had been discussing before the phone rang. He was just starting to say, "About my mother, was she—" when Mrs. Thornton interrupted and said, "Something has come up, I'm afraid, Gibson. So we'll have to cut our conversation short for now. Perhaps we can have another visit some-day. There are still so many things I want to find out about."

Gib felt the same way. There were so many things he wanted, desperately needed, to ask about. As he got to his feet Mrs. Thornton said, "About school, Gibson. Since summer vacation will begin so soon, there wouldn't be much point in your starting here in Longford just now. But next fall . . ." She paused, breathed deeply, and then went on, "But next fall—well, we'll have to decide what to do by next fall, won't we?"

That was all, except just before he went out the door she called him back to give him the gloves Miss Hooper had found. They were beautiful gloves, made of thick, soft leather, with air holes on the back and two white buttons at the wrists. They looked like they'd just about fit him, but they weren't men's gloves, and they weren't meant for shoveling manure, that was for certain.

"I know," Mrs. Thornton said, smiling ruefully. "They're ladies gloves. But they'll have to do until Hoop can get into town to do some shopping for us."

As Gib stared at the gloves she added, "And tell Hy that if he teases you about them, I'll have his hide. You go on down to the cabin now and you can also tell Hy that you aren't to do any more shoveling today. Tell him I said so."

Gib said thanks, put the gloves in his pockets, one on each side, and went out. But on the way down to the cabin he took them out and held them in his hands and thought about how Mrs. Thornton had worn them when she rode Black Silk. And how his own mother, Maggie Whittaker, had also ridden the beautiful black mare. The thought made his breath come faster. Closing his eyes, he made a picture of it, of his mother on Black Silk. The image of the mare was bright and sharp while the woman rider was blurred and distant, but there was a new and exciting certainty that everything would be much clearer very soon.

CHAPTER
20

Gib learned an awful lot during the next few days, but only about some subjects. Mrs. Thornton hadn't invited him back for another visit, so he hadn't learned anything more from her, and after that first day Hy had pretty much refused to talk about past history. At least about Gib's history. But among the subjects Hy didn't seem to mind talking about were some things about his own past. Like how his leg got busted.

"Durned motorcar did it," Hy said when Gib finally got up the nerve to ask.

Gib was impressed. "You were . . ." No, it couldn't be. "You weren't driving one, were you?" He'd heard all about motorcars, of course, and how dangerous they could be. And he'd even seen a few in Harristown, sputtering down Main Street, amazing all the people and scaring horses right out of their wits. But Gib couldn't imagine that Hy would have anything to do with a new-fangled thing like that.

Hy snorted. "Not on your life," he said. "Wouldn't catch me touchin' one of those devil wagons with a ten-foot pole. But Edgar Appleton, down at what used to be the Longford Livery Stable, he's been tryin' to sell them noisy, stinkin' machines lately, and he's been thinkin' to get the boss to buy one. Been workin' on him for a long time. I reckon he's got it in his mind that if a big-shot Longford banker like Henry Thornton was to start ridin' around in one of them contraptions, everybody in the county would buy one, even if they had to sell off half their stock and five or six kids to do it."

Hy stretched out his busted leg and rested it on the apple box he'd been using as a footstool. He stared off into space again, leaving Gib shuffling from one foot to the other, fretting to hear the rest of the story.

Finally Hy blinked, caught his breath like someone just waking up from a catnap, and took up right where he left off. "Well sir, just last month, soon as the roads dried out a bit, old Appleton took it into his head to drive out here in one of them things and take the Thorntons for a ride. And, just my luck, when he rode that smokin', rat-tlin', backfirin' bucket of bolts down our driveway I happened to be out in front of the house untyin' the boss's team from the hitchin' rail. And you can just bet it scared the holy hallelujah out of them old buggy horses. Specially Caesar. Spooky bonehead's always been real noise-shy." Hy sighed again and went quiet, gazing off into the past.

"And so what happened?" Gib prodded him.

"Ran right over me, they did," he said at last. "Buggy and all. Busted my leg in two places."

"The team ran over you!" Gib couldn't keep the shock and consternation out of his voice. "That's awful."

"Surely is," Hy said mournfully, but then he grinned. "But on the good side"—he rolled his eyes meaningfully—"it gave us a real good bargainin' chip for—" He stopped suddenly, shrugged, and changed the subject. And Gib wasn't able to get him to change it back.

Gib had also learned during those first days exactly what was expected of him as a farm-out at the Thorntons' Rocking M, or, as Hy called it, "what's left of the Rocking M." By the third day Gib had pretty much learned not only what chores he was expected to do every day but also exactly how to do them. Right at first Hy had followed him around, "showin' him the ropes," as he called it. But as soon as Gib knew where all the tools and grooming equipment were kept, and just how and when to do the feeding and stall cleaning and gardening, Hy started spending less time giving advice and more time back at the cabin resting his bad leg.

So Gib milked and watered and hoed and shoveled and fed in the morning, and then after the noon meal he did a lot more of the same. And just about when he was finishing everything up it was time to start listening for the jangle and clop that meant Mr. Thornton and Livy were returning from Longford, and there was the team to take care of.

Hy had mentioned that after his leg was broken, and before Gib had showed up, Mr. Thornton had managed to unharness the team himself for a while. But not anymore. "Don't think the boss likes being around horses much," Hy said. "And I reckon he figured a banker ought to quit doing barnyard work as soon as the outfit had an able-bodied horse wrangler again." Hy grinned at Gib. Gib didn't see what being a banker had to do with not taking care of a tired team, but to tell the truth he got a kick out of doing anything that had to do with horses, just as he'd liked taking care of old Juno back at Lovell House. And he surely didn't mind being called the wrangler, even if Hy was only pulling his leg when he said it.

So it was a part of Gib's job to fetch the tired, sweated-up team around to the barn, unharness them from the buggy, walk them a bit to cool them down, put them in their stalls, and get them fed. But then he was free to do whatever he wanted, right up until it was time for the evening milking.

And what Gib wanted to do, of course, was spend more time with the horses. Particularly with Black Silk. At first he just hung over the stall door talking to her, but on the third day, after he'd brought in the team and Hy had gone off to the cabin, Gib decided to start grooming the black mare just like he did the other horses, even though Hy had told him not to until they got better acquainted.

But Gib felt that he and Black Silk had struck up a pretty good understanding already and he was just about sure she wouldn't give him any trouble. And besides, she looked like she needed grooming real bad. Like maybe no one had brushed her down real good since Hy broke his leg.

That first time Gib didn't take his grooming stool into the stall with him, so he couldn't reach up high enough to do a good job on her back and neck. But he did enough to find out that she liked being curried and that she could be real quiet and cooperative once she got used to you.

So the next afternoon, right after he finished bringing in the team, he got out his stool and got ready to finish the job. After pouring a little extra oats into her feed bucket, he went back out for his grooming tack. Silk snorted a little when she saw the stool, which Gib had expected, since it wasn't likely she'd ever been groomed before by somebody short enough to need one. But when Gib put the stool down slow and easy like and climbed up on it, talking to her all the while, she quieted down right away. And when he started with the currycomb she looked back at him, nodding and doing her little half nicker.

"You can say that again, Silky girl," he told her. "Bet that feels mighty fine. Looks to me like nobody's brushed you down real good for a long, long time." He was running the currycomb down her short, powerful back, watching how her black hide gleamed where the dust and straw had been cleaned away, when from behind his back a voice said, "Oh!" sharply, and then, "Does Hy know you're in there?"

Silk snorted and Gib, moving slow and easy so as not to spook the mare, turned to see a hair ribbon, a bunch of gold-streaked brown hair, and the top half of a small face above the stall door. Livy Thornton. A mouth and chin became visible a second later as Livy rose onto her tiptoes, and the bottom half of the face looked just as shocked and angry as the top. Gib nodded and smiled, but Livy went on frowning.

Gib's grin widened. "You talking to me?" he asked, keeping his voice calm and quiet.

"Of course I'm talking to you," Livy said. "Who else would I be talking to?"

Gib went back to the currying but then, thinking of all the times she obviously hadn't been speaking to him, he said, "Well, I was just wondering because I've been thinking that maybe there was some reason we weren't speaking." There was no answer for so long that Gib was beginning to wonder if she'd gone away, but then the voice came back. "You didn't answer my question, Gib Whittaker. Does Hy know you're in Black Silk's stall?"

"Well," Gib said, "to tell the truth, I didn't ask Hy about grooming her, but he's been letting me come in here to do the feeding and watering." There was no answer. Gib went on with the currycomb and brush until the left side of Silky's back was clean and gleaming. Then he got down off the stool and went around behind her, gently shoving her hindquarters to make her move over and give him room to work. Now he could see the door without turning around. Livy was still there, watching with wide eyes and a slightly open mouth.

"What's the matter?" Gib asked. "You seen a ghost or something?"

Livy closed her mouth, blinked hard, gulped, and said, "I thought she was going to kick you. When you went around behind her like that, I thought for sure she was going to kick you to death."

Gib chuckled, thinking that Livy did sound worried but at the same time maybe a little disappointed. Like maybe she was mostly just looking for some excitement. He ran the comb down the beautifully arched neck and across the mare's withers several times before he asked, "What made you think old Silky would do a thing like that?"

"Because . . ." The shakiness in Livy's voice was sounding more like anger now, instead of just excitement. "Because she's a killer."

"A killer?" Gib stopped brushing. He couldn't see how that could be the least bit true. He didn't say he didn't believe it, but he must have looked it because she went on, "She is. She is too. I know she is. I hate her. I don't like any horse much, but I hate her most of all."

Gib finished with the brush then and got down off the

stool. He walked around behind Silky again while Livy went on staring wide-eyed, and gasping a little when the mare shifted her weight on her hind feet. But Gib could tell that the weight shifting had nothing to do with kicking. Outside the stall he put the brush and comb down on the stool and, joining Livy at the door, watched while Silky pushed the last crumbs of oats around with her nose and then looked at Gib, tossed her beautiful black head, and nickered softly.

"But she is a killer." Livy's voice was a trembly whisper. "I know she is. She almost killed my mother."

Now it was Gib's turn to gape. Questions raced through his mind, questions about what Silky had done—and why. If it was true, there had to be a why. And then, suddenly, an even more startling question came to mind—about the wheelchair. About whether Black Silk had something to do with Livy's mother's wheelchair.

But Gib was still feeling for the right asking words when Livy's angry blue eyes flooded over with tears. "I hate her," she gasped, "and I hate you too. I do." She whirled around then and ran out of the barn.

CHAPTER

21

That night at supper Gib kept glancing over at Mrs. Thornton in her wheelchair while his mind turned and twisted, churning up a whole lot of questions and possible answers. Julia Thornton—or the missus, as Hy called her—smiled at him when she noticed him staring, but Livy didn't. When Olivia Thornton caught him looking at her, she only glared and turned away, like always. But her glare was different now. A little more pointed, maybe, like it was saying, "Don't you dare say anything about what I told you. Don't you dare!"

She needn't have worried, though; he wasn't about to. He grinned at her again, thinking that he'd have put her mind at ease if she hadn't made it so plain that they weren't speaking.

Later that night back in the cabin, he did get up his nerve to ask Hy about the wheelchair.

"Why's she always in that chair?" he asked. "Can't she walk at all?"

Hy eased himself down into his seat and, using both hands, lifted his broken leg up onto the apple box stool. Staring off into the past with a particularly melancholy-looking arrangement of the wrinkle gullies on his beat-up old face, Hy finally sighed and said, " 'Fraid not. From what I hear, the missus is plum paralyzed from the waist down. Surely is a sorrowful thing."

"But she hasn't always been that way," Gib said.

Hy looked at him sharply. "Who told you that?" he asked.

Gib shrugged. "You did," he said. "You told me, when you said she used to ride Black Silk."

Hy nodded. "Sure enough," he said. "I did tell you that, didn't I. Well, you're right. Julia Thornton was one of the finest horsewomen I ever seen. Come by it natural, she did, being a Merrill by birth and all. But then the accident happened—in 1903, I think it was. Leastways Livy was four or five years old." Hy's voice trailed off and he went back to staring into the past. This time nothing that Gib could say would pull him out of it. And when Gib pushed a little, saying things like "What happened?" and "What kind of an accident was it?" Hy got sharp and grumpy and said he was going to bed.

But the next day, when Gib came into the horse barn after finishing his chores, Hy was already there, leaning on his crutches outside Black Silk's stall.

"Been groomin' the mare, haven't you?" he asked, and when Gib confessed, he went on, "And she behaved herself, I reckon? Didn't give you any trouble?"

Hy seemed pleased when Gib said that Silky had been good as gold, but then he wanted to see for himself. And after Gib got through demonstrating, he seemed even more pleased and impressed. Gib was putting away the grooming tack when Hy limped into the tack room and said, "How'd you like to do some ridin' this afternoon? Just a few turns around the corral, maybe."

"Riding?" Gib couldn't keep the excitement out of his voice. "Yes sir, I'd surely like that. You meaning riding Black Silk?"

Hy chuckled. "Whoa there," he said. "Slow down a bit. Maybe Silky someday, but what I had in mind just now was Lightnin'. We'll start out with Lightnin' and see how it goes. Neither one of them's been getting any exercise lately. So we'll start you off with Lightnin' and then maybe Silky soon as I get permission from the missus. All right?"

"All right," Gib agreed, trying to keep from jumping around like a two-year-old. "All right!"

Hy pointed out Lightning's bridle and saddle blankets, but when they came to the saddles he stopped, rubbing his chin thoughtfully. There were more than a dozen saddles in the tack room. Long rows of more or less beat-up old roping saddles, leftovers from the days when the Rocking M had been a big cattle ranch. Gib looked them all over and picked out the one he thought must be Hy's, as well-worn as any, but cleaner and less stiff from lack of use.

"This what you use on Lightning?" Gib asked.

"Yep." Hy nodded. "Mine. Had them stirrup straps and fenders made special for my long legs." He glanced at Gib, shaking his head. "Don't know as how we can shorten them up enough for you." Then he stepped back and, balancing on one crutch, pointed to something way up on the top row. Right at first Gib thought he was pointing to a fancy silver-studded lady's sidesaddle. "No, not that useless contraption," Hy hooted. "The one wrapped up in the blanket. Climb up and get that one down."

It was a small but beautifully made stockman's saddle, the fine leather of the skirt and stirrup fenders heavily embossed with a pattern of leaves and vines. "Miss Julia's," Hy said, as Gib looked up at him questioningly.

Gib nodded. "But it's not a—"

"A sidesaddle." Hy made a snorting noise. "No sirree. Miss Julia—the missus, that is—grew up riding astride. Her pa said those gulldurned sidesaddles was too dangerous on a ranch. The missus never even had one until . . ."

"Until when?" Gib asked, but Hy only shook his head. "Look at them stirrup straps," he said, grinning. "Just up a notch or two'll be about right. Fit you like a glove, I'm thinkin'."

Gib thought so too. As he led Lightning out to the

140

hitching rack he was feeling excited but not scared. Not really scared, although when he thought about it afterward he didn't know why he wasn't. After all, except for sitting on old Juno a couple of times, he really hadn't been on a horse since he was a little kid, and you might just wonder if a person could forget how. But somehow he knew he hadn't. He did need a few pointers from Hy about the saddling, but once he was in the saddle, which did indeed fit him like a glove, it was all there, just as if he'd been doing it all along.

And riding Lightning was exactly like something he'd done before. After he'd been around the corral a few times, feeling the familiarity of the old horse's eager energy and quick, smooth gaits, Gib turned him back to where Hy was leaning on the fence.

Before he could get a word out, Hy said, "You knowed you'd rode the old blue before, didn't you? Came right back to you, just like it was yesterday. Every time I showed up at your ma's place you used to beg me to put you up in the saddle and let you take Lightnin' down the road a ways. But we had to be sure your mama wasn't lookin'. Thought maybe he was too much of a horse for you, she did, but I knew better." Hy rubbed Lightning's nose and chuckled. "And he recollects you riding him too, sure as shootin'. Probably's tryin' to figure how come you put on so much weight since the last time you two had a little gallop."

Hy went off to the cabin, still chuckling, and Gib went on riding Lightning until it was time to do the milking.

And from that day on he did all his morning chores moving faster than a scared jackrabbit, so as to leave more time for riding in the afternoon. He rode around the corral at first, but then he began heading out through the east gate and off across open country. Prairie country, which Hy said used to be part of the Rocking M before the boss sold it off. Riding far out across the open land, mostly at a walk or trot, he sometimes let Lightning have his head and stretch himself a little for a half mile or so.

Riding the old blue roan was one of the most comforting things Gib could ever remember doing. And using Mrs. Thornton's beautiful old saddle, which his own mother must have ridden on that time when she rode Black Silk, made it even better. At night, just thinking about those rides was enough to cure the worrying fits he got sometimes when he let his mind go to wondering about what had happened to poor old Georgie—and what was happening to Jacob and Bobby, too. Or about why Mrs. Thornton hadn't asked him in for another visit so that he could find out more about the Gibson Whittaker who had lived near the Rocking M Ranch and had known the Thorntons and an old cowhand named Hyram Carter and maybe some other folks who'd been important to him once upon a time.

Mrs. Thornton hadn't talked to him much at all after that first visit, though, and she apparently wasn't talking to Hy either, because Hy kept saying he hadn't yet had a chance to ask her if Gib could ride Black Silk.

But lately there'd been another late-night worry pestering Gib. And that was whether he was there at the Rocking M only because of Hy's broken leg, and if the Thorntons were planning to kick him out as soon as Hy got well enough to take care of things by himself, the way he'd done before.

Gib tried to convince himself that couldn't be what the Thorntons had in mind. Not if Buster had been right when he said that the official papers promised that the signers would keep any farmed-out kid they took until he was eighteen years old. Whatever you might think about Mr. Thornton, Gib told himself, it didn't seem like he was the type to welch on an official paper. But still, now that he knew what being a Thornton farm-out was like, with the good food and the horses—particularly the horses—Gib didn't like to think about being kicked out. So that was another thing he had to put out of his mind at night by reliving his afternoon rides on Lightning.

In the meantime other things were happening in the life of Gib Whittaker, the farmed-out kid. The blisters on his hands had healed up, for one thing, and stayed that way because of the gloves. Mrs. Thornton's riding gloves at first and then, after Miss Hooper got into town to do some shopping, some small men's work gloves. And while she was at it she got him some denim trousers and a pair of stockman's boots. Miss Hooper said he was going to have a new suit too, just as soon as she finished sewing it up.

Getting to know Miss Hooper better was another one of the things that was happening that month. And one of the surprises, too. When Gib had seen Miss Hooper pushing Mrs. Thornton's chair into the dining room that first evening, he'd thought she was a sure enough head-mistress type, bone-thin and stiff-necked, with a frown that could make your hair stand on end. But when you got to know her she wasn't that way at all.

When you got to know Miss Hooper you found out that talking to her was a lot like talking to Hy, except for the good grammar, of course. She had a way of glaring at you that you weren't really supposed to take seriously, and she liked to say shocking things like "Go behind that screen and take those pants off," and then, when Gib stared and gulped, "Heavens to Betsy, boy. Just want you to try this on for size. Nobody's going to look at you."

She tended to say things like that quite a lot, things that got your attention in a hurry and then turned out not to mean what they seemed to. So far they'd mostly talked about blisters and gloves and denim pants, but Gib had a feeling she might be the one who'd talk about some more important things once they got better ac-quainted.

So May turned into June and Gib went on spending most of his time taking care of the Thorntons' garden and barnyard critters, and all the rest of his time with the horses. One day for Gib was pretty much like the other, except for Sundays, of course. Sundays were easier be-cause milking and feeding were his only chores. No gar-dening or stall cleaning on Sunday. But no church either, at least not for Gib. The Thorntons went to church every

144

Sunday morning, except in real bad weather, and sometimes Mrs. Perry and Miss Hooper went too. But Hy stayed home and so did Gib. Nobody asked Gib if he wanted to go, but even if they had he would have had a hard time choosing church over all that extra time with the horses.

In June the Longford school let out for the summer, so Livy was staying home and Mr. Thornton was leaving later in the mornings. But even though Livy Thornton was home all day now, Gib didn't see much of her except at meals.

Then one afternoon when he was riding Lightning around in the big corral, which was quite close to the house, he happened to look up, and there she was sitting on the roof of the veranda. There was something about the way she was sitting, with her arms wrapped around her tucked-up knees, that made him feel sure she'd been watching him for quite a spell.

CHAPTER

22

She was there the next day too, and the next. The roof where Livy sat went out over the side veranda and could be reached from a second-floor window. So it was an easy place to go if you wanted to have a good look at what was going on in the big corral. But the question Gib started asking himself was why.

Gib wondered a lot about that. Why would a girl, or anybody else for that matter, waste half the afternoon watching somebody taking an old cowhorse through his paces? Nothing at all fancy, just a lot of walking, trotting, galloping, and now and then a short run. It wasn't much to watch, particularly if you were a person who didn't like horses in general, and especially if you hated the person who was doing the riding.

And Livy Thornton surely did hate him. Ever since she'd told him so, she'd gone right on making it clear every time they met, tossing her head and glaring whenever she caught his eye, and going out of her way to keep from having to speak to him. He didn't know why she hated him, unless it was just that being around sorry people, like tramps and farmed-out orphans, made her feel depressed. That might be it, of course, but then why didn't she just ignore him instead of working herself up into a lather like she'd done that day in the barn? Gib was wondering about that on that third day when he crossed the end of the corral nearest the house and there she was again, staring down at him.

Nothing about it was particularly funny, but Gib felt a grin coming on. Pulling up on the reins and at the same time nudging Lightning a bit with his heels, he set the old pony to dancing a little. And then, as they pranced past Livy's roost with Lightning tossing his head and stepping sideways, Gib did a big wave and pretended to tip an imaginary sombrero.

And Livy smiled and waved back. At least he thought she did. Lightning had chosen that moment to circle to the right, so Gib hadn't had time to get a real good look, but he was pretty sure that the last thing he saw was a smile and a wave.

That night in his creaky cot in the loft of Hy's cabin, Gib had something else to put his mind to before he went to sleep. In between his usual worries, he also spent some time trying to decide if Livy really had smiled and waved. And if she had—why? He couldn't seem to come up with any answers, so after a while he put it out of his mind and concentrated on looking forward to tomorrow and his next ride on Lightning. Only, as it turned out, it wasn't the blue roan he rode that next day.

When Gib came into the barn that afternoon Hy was already there waiting for him with a big grin on his face. "Hey there, bronc buster," he said when he saw Gib. "Just talked to the missus and she said you can start riding the mare. Said she'd go by my judgment, and if I thought you were ready, it was fine with her. Said she'd been worrying about Silky not gettin' any exercise and she'd be right glad to have the problem taken care of."

For a moment Gib couldn't believe his ears. His eyes locked on Hy's grinning face, he ran over the words Hy was saying a couple of times to be sure they meant what he thought they did. As soon as he was sure, he went over to the stall and called her name. And when she came, nickering and snuffling at his arm and the side of his face, he whispered the good news in her ear before he and Hy headed down to the tack room.

Black Silk's bridle was made of top-grade black leather and studded with time-tarnished silver stars.

"Stars," Gib said, "like on the sidesaddle."

"That useless thing," Hy grunted. "That was just so she could dress like a lady. Miss Julia grew up ridin' in plain old trousers here on the ranch, and one of them divided skirts when she went into town. But after she got married she started using that thing. Guess the boss thought it was more fittin', her being a banker's wife and all. Had that lopsided contraption on Silky the day . . ." Hy glanced at Gib then and kind of ran down.

"On what day?" Gib asked. But Hy only shrugged and said, "That there saddle you been usin' is the one Miss Julia's pa had made for her when she wasn't much older than you are now."

Black Silk was very mannerly about being saddled up, taking the bit without any struggle and not even humping her back when the cinch was pulled tight. "See there," Hy said, patting the shiny black neck, "sweet-handlin' as a lamb. Like I always said, not a mean bone in her body." He looked at Gib. "But's that not to say she's an easy ride. Full of fire, she is, and bustin' with energy. And she'll be specially full of it today, not having been worked for so long. Think you better lead her over to the corral afore you mount up, and then keep her walkin' till you feel her settlin' down." He smiled and nodded. "You'll know when," he said. "You'll feel it."

Gib did feel it. Right at first, riding Black Silk was a lot like sitting on a big jackrabbit. High-stepping and full of bounce and fire, she danced around the corral like she was just playing with gravity. Like she could have climbed right up through the air if she hadn't been held back by the bit in her mouth. She was soft-mouthed, though, and quick to obey the reins as long as the hands holding them knew how to make them talk. And after the talking had gone on for a while, the dancing settled down and the two of them moved smoothly together, around and around the corral at a sensible walk, a trot, and then a controlled, rocking-chair gallop. But all the while Gib could feel the hot-blooded urge to run surging just under the surface of all Hy's good training.

"Good girl, good girl," he kept crooning softly. "Easy now, take it real easy."

Busy as he was keeping a lid on all that hot blood, it took Gib quite a while to remember to see if Livy was watching. But as soon as he did he looked up, and there she was, sitting on the roof just like before. And behind her, at the open window, he could just make out another face, or maybe two. Turning Silky back, he rode her up close to the fence. Sure enough, the faces behind the window belonged to Mrs. Thornton and Miss Hooper. When Gib waved, they both waved back, and so did Livy. As if feeling Gib's excitement, Silky came up against the bit dancing and tossing her head, and it took him halfway around the ring to settle her back down. Later, when Gib was cooling out the mare and rubbing her down, he could still feel the dancing in his own bones.

That night, as they were going in for the evening meal, Hy stopped Gib and said, "I wouldn't talk about riding Silky if I were you. Leastways not unless anybody asks you."

Gib was surprised. "You already told me about that," he said. "About not talking at meals unless somebody asks me something."

Hy nodded, chuckling. "I know," he said. "Just

thought you might think to say somethin' this once, it being sort of a special occasion and all." He stopped smiling then and shrugged. "Just thought you ought to know that it wouldn't be a good idea to mention it when the boss is around."

"Doesn't he know?" Gib asked. "Doesn't he know I rode her?"

"Oh, I reckon he knows, all right," Hy said. "But I got a feeling he wouldn't want to hear about it. Mare's kind of a sore point with the boss."

During supper that evening Mr. Thornton read his paper, as usual, and didn't look at Gib at all. Mrs. Thornton and Miss Hooper didn't say anything to him either—not with words, at least. But they both gave Gib looks and smiles that said a lot. Livy, though, had gone back to pretending she didn't know he was alive.

CHAPTER

23

Summer came on fast that year, the sun rising hot and clear before Gib had even finished the morning milking. Working in the garden, harvesting now as well as hoeing and watering, Gib wore a big old ten-gallon hat, but even so the skin on his face went from pale palomino to pretty close to bay in no time at all. As for exercising the horses, Silky one day and Lightning the next, he took to doing that mostly after supper. Trotting and galloping around the corral as the sun sank below the horizon and the long, slow summer twilight faded into night, he sometimes wished he could ride right on through till morning instead of going back to try to sleep in the sweltering cabin.

The sun, beating down through the long summer days, turned the whole cabin into an oven, especially the loft. Gib took to bringing his blankets down the ladder and making a bed on the cabin floor. Which was some cooler but a lot noisier, what with Hy's sighing and snoring and moaning just a few feet away.

Hy's moaning worried Gib some, and sure enough it turned out that his busted leg wasn't healing up the way it ought to. Halfway through July Mr. Thornton took a day off to take Hy into Harristown to the hospital, and when they came back Hy had a new cast on his leg.

"Durn thing was healing up crooked," he told Gib. "Doc had to break it again and start all over."

"Break it again." Gib's hair prickled at the back of his neck at the notion of breaking someone's leg on purpose—did they do it with a hammer, or maybe just stomp on it? It was something that didn't bear thinking about. "How'd they do that?" he asked Hy warily, his face squinched up against the pain of hearing about it. And at the same time trying to shut his mind to the selfish thought that now he wouldn't have to worry about being sent away because he wasn't needed at the Rocking M. Not for a while, anyway.

Hy didn't want to talk about how they'd done it. Instead he just asked how Silky had behaved that day, and Gib was glad to change to a new subject. Particularly when the new one was Black Silk.

"She was just fine," he told Hy. "Oh, she frets a little when we're galloping. Trying to talk me into letting her run, I guess. You think I could let her go full out soon? Just a couple of turns round the corral? I think I could handle it."

Hy shrugged. "I ain't worried about you not being able

153

to handle it. I knowed all along that you had a good ear for horse lingo, Gibby, but I been right surprised the way you've gentled that mare into doin' whatever you ask her to. But about lettin' her run, it's just that the corral's hardly big enough for her to really stretch herself. Needs a real racetrack, she does. It's what them hot-blooded horses are bred for."

Gib had heard about the mare being from Kentucky before. "Did she really come from Kentucky?" he asked.

"Surely did. Old Dan Merrill, Miss Julia's pa—" He paused, grinning. "—the missus's pa, that is, promised her a Kentucky Thoroughbred as a weddin' present. But the one he was dickerin' for didn't work out, and then Dan died, and things got put off some more. Warn't till three or four year later that the mare finally turned up. Just a yearlin', and no more than halter-broke, but just about the prettiest thing I ever did see. Easy to train, too. Smart as could be and full of fire, but right out front about it. Not a bit mean or sneaky."

Hy's eyes had that backward stare to them and his voice had an inward drift, as if he was just talking to himself. Gib sat very still, not even allowing his mouth to twitch or his eyes to blink, for fear that if Hy noticed how curious he was, he'd clam up again and not go on about the training of Black Silk—and maybe about what she'd had to do with Mrs. Thornton's accident.

But it didn't work. Suddenly Hy blinked, nodded, and started in about horses he had known that really *were* sneaky, and how a "big old rawboned sorrel I owned once't always was tryin' to edge you up to a fence where he could snag your leg on the barb wire." Gib was disappointed. Hy's horse stories were always interesting, but some were a lot more so than others. Particularly the ones that were about Black Silk.

By August, Hy was letting Gib take Black Silk out onto the prairie, where he could let her show what she could do. But only after they'd been out for a while, trotting and galloping and "takin' the edge off," as Hy put it. Even so, running the black mare was an experience like nothing else Gib had ever done.

The split second he loosened the reins and touched her ribs with his heels, she shot forward like a cannonball. Her run was sweet and smooth, and faster than the prairie wind. Leaning forward to cut the wind, Gib thrilled to her speed and strength, but even more to the feel of the mare's glory in doing what she was born to do.

Gib gloried in the running too, but after it was over the feeling it left was more a kind of quieting. In riding Silky, whether out on the open prairie or in the corral, Gib found a quieting he couldn't seem to find anywhere else, not even in the midst of one of his best daydreams. He didn't know why. Part of it was just the way he'd always felt about any horse, but multiplied over and over again by Black Silk's beauty and strength and courage. And multiplied another time by the way the mare related to him and accepted what he asked of her, even when it was just to line herself up against the corral gate quickly and neatly, so he could lean down and reach the latch.

One afternoon in late August Gib saddled up earlier than usual and headed for the corral. His free time was starting early that day because he didn't have to wait to take care of the team when Mr. Thornton came home. At breakfast that morning Mr. Thornton had said, "By the way, Hy, the team won't be back this afternoon. I have business in Harristown today and if it lasts until dark I'll likely have to stay in town for the night."

Mr. Thornton had been talking to Hy when he said that, even though Gib was standing right beside him and it was Gib who actually took care of the team. It was always that way. Mr. Thornton gave Gib his orders by talking to Hy, and then Hy would tell Gib what the boss had said. Gib didn't know why, but it kind of looked like Mr. Thornton didn't want to have anything to do with him. Then again, maybe it was just because he thought Gib was too young to remember. You couldn't be sure about things like that.

Either way, it was all right with Gib. And having the extra time off that afternoon was more than all right. It was a nice day, warm but not blazing hot, and he was looking forward to a fine time riding, first in the corral and then maybe out on the prairie. But just as Gib and the eagerly dancing black mare reached the corral gate he heard voices and turned to see Miss Hooper and Mrs. Thornton. Mrs. Thornton was in her chair and Miss

Hooper was pushing it across the barnyard toward the corral.

Wondering if something was wrong—he'd never seen either of them in the barnyard before—he was turning Silk toward them when Miss Hooper called, "Go on in. Take her on into the corral." She pointed then and said, "The chair."

Gib took her meaning right away. Silky could be real spooky about large objects that didn't stay put—like wheelbarrows, for instance—and she'd probably feel the same way about a wheelchair. So he opened the gate, went on in, and started putting Silky through her paces. The two women came slowly and quietly across the yard to where they could get a good view between the rails of the corral fence. Gib took Silky around the ring, showing off her gaits and the way she responded to the reins, turning on a dime and backing straight and true.

It wasn't until they'd been around the ring a few times that he began to notice a difference in the way Silky was behaving. The difference was that every time they got anywhere near the two women Silky turned toward them, testing the air, flipping her ears, and edging in their direction. Finally Gib pulled her to a stop a few feet away and said, "She wants to come over there, ma'am. Shall I let her?"

"Yes, yes, let her," Mrs. Thornton said quickly, and the moment Black Silk heard her voice her ears flicked forward and she nickered. And when Mrs. Thornton put her hand through the fence Black Silk ran her velvety lips over the hand and went right on nickering, a soft, low sound that Gib had never heard her make before. Gib heard Mrs. Thornton say some gentle, crooning things, but suddenly her voice kind of stumbled and she said, "Take me back, Hoop. Take me away." Miss Hooper quickly pulled the chair back and pushed it toward the house. And Gib could see that Mrs. Thornton had her hands over her face and her shoulders were shaking.

There were only five people at supper that night. Olivia had gone to visit a friend in Longford, so there were only Hy and Gib and the three women, Mrs. Perry, Miss Hooper, and Mrs. Thornton. The food was great, as always, but nothing else was quite the same. For one thing, there was a lot more talking. Miss Hooper and Mrs. Thornton chatted a lot about the old times, when Mrs. Thornton was Julia Merrill, the Rocking M was the biggest ranch in the county, and Miss Hooper had come to live at the ranch to be Miss Julia's teacher and governess.

There was also some talk about Gib himself. About how he, as Mrs. Thornton put it, "had a real gift with horses. Hy tells me he's never seen anything quite like it," she went on. "Almost like you spoke the language."

Gib felt his face get hot, but it was something he surely liked hearing. "Wish I could," he said. "I'd like that a whole lot."

It was right about then that Mrs. Thornton said how glad she was to see someone getting some use out of her old saddle. "Fits you as if it were made for you," she said, and smiled. "Anyway, Gibson, from now on it's yours."

Hy did a lot of talking that night, too. He started out just answering questions about the old days, but before long he was carrying on like he always did back in the cabin. Telling long stories that started out, "Well, that must of took place way back in the summer of . . ."

Gib wanted to talk about Black Silk. Only he didn't, because he didn't want Mrs. Thornton to cry again. But when he and Hy were on their way back to the cabin that night, suddenly, without any prodding, Hy began to talk and talk and talk.

CHAPTER

24

"'Twasn't no way the mare's fault," Hy said. "Big part of it was mine. I should have throwed a holy fit when they first started talkin' about the missus ridin' in that there parade. I did tell them a Fourth of July parade weren't no place for a hot-blooded, half-broke filly, but nobody paid me no heed. But a lot more of it was his fault for buying her that death-dealing sidesaddle and telling her she had to use it whenever she went into town." Hy didn't say who "he" was, but Gib was pretty sure he knew.

"Silky stood it pretty well, I guess, until they were right downtown. But then the band started up just as some crazy hoodlums ran past real close, yellin' and whoopin' and pulling a cart they'd fixed up to look like a fire engine." Hy stopped and sighed before he went on. "She didn't buck, she fell. Reared up and slipped on an oily patch and just went on over backwards. Miss Julia could have handled it real easy if she'd been in her regular saddle and wearing trousers—kicked her feet loose and jumped clear, like I taught her when she was just a tyke. But as it was . . ." His voice trailed off and he went into one of his blank-eyed stares. Gib waited, nudging him now and then with "Hy?" and "What happened then, Hy?"

When he came out of it, Hy's face had darkened. "Wanted to shoot the mare, he did. Would have, too, 'cept Miss Julia made him promise he wouldn't. I don't know how she got him to promise, but he did. But Silky's been a sore point ever since. I went on with her trainin' and kept her exercised and all, right up till I busted my leg, but the boss won't even look at her if he can help it." Shaking his head, Hy grinned ruefully.

"When he writ out the things you were supposed to do, all the chores he wanted you to handle in one day, there warn't one word about Black Silk. Everything else on the spread you was supposed to feed and water and clean up after, but he didn't put down a durn thing about the mare. Like he wouldn't care if we let her starve to death."

"But he must know we aren't letting her starve," Gib said. "And he knows I've been exercising her. He never comes out of the house when I'm riding her, but he must know about it."

"He knows," Hy said. "He's just not going to look at it. The boss handles all kinds of things he don't like that way. Just kind of looks the other way."

Gib nodded, thinking how he himself was one of the things Mr. Thornton looked the other way about, pretty much like he did about Black Silk. He didn't know why, but that surely seemed to be the way things were.

The season changed soft and easy that fall, at least at first. Gib went on with his usual chores and spent a bunch of extra time harvesting in the garden and orchard, bringing in all the fall fruits and vegetables for Mrs. Perry to put up in bottles or store away in the root cellar.

When September came Hy finally got the cast off his leg, but he walked real careful with a cane, as if his leg was still hurting him some. And Gib went on doing most of the chores.

Then school started. No one said a word to Gib about school starting, but Livy began to ride into town with her father again, all dressed up in her school clothes and carrying her book bag. And in bed at night Gib took to thinking about school and the things he'd been pretty good at, like reading and writing, and wondering whether he'd ever have a chance to be good at them again.

But then one day right after breakfast, when no one else happened to be in the kitchen, Miss Hooper asked him to come into the library as soon as he finished his work that afternoon. Gib got all excited, thinking that Mrs. Thornton had finally decided to talk to him again and wondering if she'd tell him some more about his mother. But when he got to the library no one was there except Miss Hooper. When he came into the room she frowned at him the way she always did and told him to turn around.

"Heavens to Betsy, boy," she said. "You're growing like a weed. At this rate you're going to be needing new clothes in no time. And I promised you wouldn't be needing anything more this year."

"Promised?" Gib asked.

Miss Hooper put her hands on her hips and frowned harder with her head tipped to one side. "Aren't you the sly one with your sneaky questions. 'Promised whom?' you're asking." She sighed and said, "I think you know the answer, and I think you know who thinks you shouldn't be given the notion an education was any part of that Lovell House contract."

Gib nodded, and she nodded back. "He says he intends to let you attend school off and on, when things are especially slow here on the ranch, but in the meantime . . ." Miss Hooper picked up a canvas book bag and handed it to Gib. "In the meantime," she repeated, "see what you can do with these."

The bag was full of books. Books on history and geography and arithmetic, and even some storybooks, like *Tom Sawyer* by Mark Twain and *Treasure Island* by Robert Louis Stevenson. Gib had read *Tom Sawyer* before but would be glad to read it over and over again, and he'd never before read *Treasure Island*. At the bottom of the sack there were some tablets and pencils and a big bag of candles.

Almost every night from then on Gib read and studied for at least an hour or two by candlelight. He worked at the table until Hy began to grumble about the light, saying it was "way past bedtime for workin' folks." And then he went on reading up in the loft with the candle on a box near the head of his cot.

He liked reading in the loft for a lot of reasons. For one thing, he could read until he was already nearly asleep, so all he had to do was blow out the candle and he was dead to the world in half a minute, instead of going through a long spell of thinking and worrying about one thing and another. About what was happening to Georgie and Jacob and Bobby, for instance, or about why Mrs. Thornton hadn't let him visit her again to talk about who Gib Whittaker was and where he came from.

Another reason he liked studying in the loft was a little brown field mouse who'd started hanging around because of the crumbs in Gib's pockets. Crumbs that came from the cookies Mrs. Perry gave Gib to "hold him over." "Here, take these," Mrs. Perry had taken to saying when Gib was leaving the kitchen after breakfast. "Hardworking boy like you needs something to hold him over."

So the mouse started hanging around looking for cookie crumbs, and before long Gib had him tamed and trained to eat right out of his hand. He named the mouse

Bobby, after nervous, skittery old Bobby Whitestone, and he was real good company.

So Gib studied an hour or two every night, at Hy's table first and then up in the loft with the Bobby mouse. Mostly he worked through the hard parts of the arithmetic by himself, but two or three times, when there was something that he just couldn't figure out, he managed to let Miss Hooper know and she arranged a quick meeting in the library to put him on the right track.

It was a strange thing, but somehow the late-night studying was—well, maybe not fun exactly, but a little bit exciting. A lot more exciting, for instance, than studying at Lovell House had ever been. Gib didn't know why, except there was something secret and risky about learning up there in the loft. After he'd learned each new thing he felt a kind of sneaky satisfaction that, even if he had to stop tomorrow, he'd gotten one more little bit stashed away where no one could ever take it from him.

So the days passed and the first killing frost came and there was no more to be done in the garden, but work in the barn and chicken house and cow shed went on, and Gib went on riding Lightning or Silky almost every afternoon, and reading and studying almost every night. Hy grumbled a lot about the waste of candles, but he did start doing the morning milking so Gib could sleep in a little longer after a late night with his books.

And Miss Hooper went on providing Gib not only with books, but also with other things like a heavy coat and some warmer gloves. The gloves were thick and soft and Gib took extra good care of them, putting them away in a safe place every night, and thinking about Georgie every time he pulled them on over his cold hands before he went out into the freezing air.

It wasn't until early in December that the cold turned really hard and mean. In the chicken house the old hens huddled together and roused themselves only to eat and then drink hastily when Gib broke the ice on their water pans. And in the barns the horses nickered plaintively, as if blaming their human caretakers for their discomfort. Even old Bessie, the milk cow, got cross and nervy, shaking her horns at Gib as if to scold him for the awful weather.

Hy got out horse blankets for Silky and Lightning. For Silky because she was a fine lady, he said, and for Lightning because he was an old man. But Caesar and Comet had to do without. There weren't any more blankets, and besides, the bays were prairie stock and they could take it.

Mr. Thornton went on driving through the bitter cold to Longford almost every day, but Livy had quit going in with him. Instead she was going to school in the library, and starting on a Monday in early December, Gib was too.

That first day when Livy came into the library carrying her book bag she was wearing a plain gingham dress instead of one of the fancy things she wore on Longford school days, and her golden brown hair was braided in pigtails instead of twisted into long corkscrew curls. Gib glanced at her out of the corner of his eye; she did the same at him, and then she marched up to where Miss Hooper was sitting and whispered in her ear. Gib didn't hear exactly what she said, but it looked to be some kind of question.

But Miss Hooper's answer was right out loud even though Livy shook her head and glared, trying to make her shush. "Why, I guess it was my idea, my dear," she said. "But your mother agreed that as long as I was going to have to spend my days playing schoolmarm again I might as well have two students instead of just one. Make myself twice as useful."

Still glaring at Miss Hooper, Livy flounced into a chair at the other end of the library table from Gib and began to take out her books and bang them down. She didn't say anything at all to Gib during the lessons, but when he answered some of Miss Hooper's questions about the Constitutional Convention and got the right answer to a real doozy of a long division problem, he noticed she was staring at him in a puzzled way.

Gib tried not to grin, but he felt like it, especially when he looked at Miss Hooper and she gave him the especially fierce frown that always had some kind of joke behind it. This time the joke was that the Constitution questions came from the chapter Miss Hooper had had him read just the night before, and the arithmetic problem was one she'd just helped him with. They had geography next, which had always been one of Gib's favorite subjects. Gib was sorry when Miss Hooper gave out the homework assignments and said, "Well, I don't know about you infants, but the old schoolmarm's worn to a frazzle. Class dismissed. Teacher's off to have herself a nap." When she left the room Gib was still copying the homework page numbers and Livy was standing at her end of the table staring at him. He finished packing up his books before he looked back.

She wasn't smiling. Just that round-eyed stare, but as he turned to go she said, "You're smart."

It was the first time she'd spoken to him since she'd yelled she hated him that day in the barn.

CHAPTER

25

After that first day in what Miss Hooper had started calling "The Rocking M Institution of Higher Learning," things began to change a bit. Once Livy got started speaking to Gib she kind of overdid it. Especially when Miss Hooper asked Gib a question and Miss Olivia Thornton thought she knew a better answer.

"Miss Hooper, Miss Hooper," she'd say, shaking her hand in the air, "that's not right. I know the answer. Let me tell it."

Sometimes Miss Hooper would let them argue it out, like the time Gib said that the Civil War was about saving the union and Livy said, "No it wasn't. It was about freeing the slaves." Livy started quoting Miss Albert, her teacher at the Longford School, and so Gib quoted Miss Mooney. He was glad when Miss Hooper said they were both partly correct, but he could tell Livy didn't like it much. Livy was partial to winning arguments outright.

But she only pouted for a few minutes before she got over it and went back to being her normal self. And later, when Miss Hooper had gone out to get herself a cup of tea, Livy asked Gib about Miss Mooney.

"What was her name, that teacher you had at the orphanage?"

Gib got up to put away the encyclopedia he'd been using. "Miss Mooney," he said over his shoulder.

"Oh yes, Miss Mooney." Livy scribbled something down in her notebook, as if she was making sure to remember Miss Mooney's name. When she had finished she asked, "Did she whip you a lot? I mean, did she whip all the kids?"

Gib shook his head, grinning at the thought of Miss Mooney whipping anybody. "No," he said. "She didn't whip anybody."

Livy's eyes narrowed suspiciously. "I thought all the teachers whipped people at that orphanage. I heard all the boys at Lovell House got whipped every day."

"Where'd you hear that?"

Livy shrugged. "Oh, everywhere. The kids at school said so. They said that all you orphans got whipped and starved and frozen and—"

She paused suddenly and stared at Gib. "What?" she asked. "What is it?"

"Frozen?" Gib said. His face had a stiff feel to it, as if it had suddenly frozen, too. "Where'd you hear about somebody getting frozen?"

Livy looked at him sharply, and when she spoke, her

voice had a different sound to it. Softer and more serious. "It was in the paper. In *The Longford Journal* and the Harristown papers too. About the boy from the orphanage who got loaned out to a mean old man who sent him out in a blizzard without any gloves. They talked about it at our church a lot. Our Sunday school class prayed for him and when he died we took up a collection to . . ." She stopped. "Gib? Gib? What's the matter?"

He was sitting at the table again without knowing how he got there, his head on his arms, while a painful tornado of grief and pity whirled through his head. "Georgie," he said. "He died? Georgie's dead?"

"Oh, Gib," Livy said. "Did you know him? You did, didn't you?" And when Gib nodded, "Oh, Gib. I'm sorry."

After that day Gib and Livy talked to each other whenever they got the chance. Whenever Miss Hooper left for a minute to get tea or a different book, or at the end of the school day, Livy would start right in, talking as hard and fast as she could. So Gib talked too, not quite as fast, maybe, but he had a lot to say as well. At first it was mostly about Georgie.

Gib wanted to know how and why Georgie died. "Miss Offenbacher said he was doing as well as could be expected," he told Livy. "And then we never heard anything more. We didn't see any newspapers for a while, but we hardly ever got to see newspapers, so we didn't know that was why." He stopped and swallowed hard. "Did they cut off his hands?" he made himself ask as, against his will, his own hands crept up to grasp his wrists. "Is that why he died?"

Livy shook her head. "I'm not sure about his hands. The paper didn't say. The paper said he died of pneumonia."

"I hope they didn't cut off his hands," Gib said over the hot, throbbing lump in his throat that made it hard for him to say anything at all. "He was so scared they would."

Livy didn't talk for a while either. And when Gib looked over to see why, he saw she was crying. He turned his eyes away quickly, but when he got his voice back and began to tell her about how they had found Georgie in Juno's stall, she cried harder than ever. Then they just sat there for a long time not looking at each other. At least, Gib didn't look at Livy, because watching her cry made it harder for him to keep from crying, too. She was still crying when they heard the sound of the buggy in the driveway. Livy ran out to wash her face, and Gib hurriedly put on his coat and went out through the kitchen and around to the front of the house to get the team and take them to the barn.

The next day when Miss Hooper went to get tea Livy wanted to hear some more about Georgie, and so Gib told her how he'd always sort of taken care of Georgie because he was kind of helpless, and how some people called him Rabbit Olson. He also told her about the time he'd set Georgie straight when Elmer was trying to scare him to death about a bloodsucking ghost that was supposed to live in Lovell House. And Livy told Gib about how the paper said that a judge had decided that Mr. Bean couldn't have any more boys from Lovell House or from any other orphanage.

"He'd had a lot of boys working for him before," Livy said. "Older boys. But they always got fed up and ran away."

And Gib said that was probably why he'd picked Georgie even though he was pretty young and small to be chosen for a farm-out. Livy agreed with him. "That murdering old slave driver must have thought that poor Georgie would be too scared to run away," she said.

Livy said that Mr. Bean's farm was right there in Longford County and that he used to come into town sometimes to buy supplies, but after everyone found out about Georgie, old Bean quit coming because nobody in town would talk to him.

"Serves him right," Gib said. And Livy, with her eyes shooting blue fire the way they did when she was really mad, said, "Except not bad enough. What he should have been is *hung*." So that was one thing they agreed on. That Mr. Bean should have been hung, or at least thrown into prison for life. But that turned out to be one of the few things they agreed on a hundred percent.

As the lessons continued they disagreed on a lot of things, like for instance what was the longest river in the world or the highest mountain. Sometimes it seemed to Gib that whatever answer he gave to one of Miss Hooper's questions, Livy was bound and determined to give a different one. And when it turned out that he was right, which happened quite a lot, she always had some excuse. One of her excuses was that Gib was older than she was, so she didn't have a fair chance.

"Not a lot older," Gib told her once, grinning a little. That was a mistake. The grinning, that is. Livy didn't like to be grinned at.

She glared at him. "Yes, you are," she said. "A lot older. You must be. What year were you born?"

And when Gib said he was born in 1897, she said, "See? I wasn't born until 1898. So you're a whole year older than I am."

"What month is your birthday, my dear?" Miss Hooper asked, and when Livy said April, she went on, "And I believe Gibson was born in December. Isn't that right, Gib? So that makes him about four months older, doesn't it?"

Livy glared and in her poutiest voice said, "Well, he's bigger anyhow, and his head's bigger. So that means he ought to have a lot more room for brains than I've got."

Gib couldn't help laughing at that, and so did Miss Hooper, and after a while Livy's lips twitched and she laughed, too.

CHAPTER

26

That winter there was a terrible blizzard in the month of December. It started on the fifteenth and raged all day on the sixteenth, which was Gib's birthday. Early in the morning of the fifteenth there had been only a cold, gray hush in the air, but Hy had seen what was coming. "A real ripsnorter's blowin' up," he told Gib.

They were on their way to the barn at the time and Gib asked, "Is it because of the color of the sky? Is that how you know?"

And Hy said, "Well, that too, but mostly because my busted bones start achin'. When a blizzard's blowin' up, every durned bone of mine that ever got busted goes to achin' like a bad tooth."

Gib looked at Hy and shook his head, thinking about all those aching bones. Not just the ones the team ran over, either. According to Hy, nearly every bone in his body had been busted at one time or another. Mostly when he was a young cowhand and his job had been to green-break wild mustangs for the Rocking M. "Right in off the open range," he always said. "Some of them never had a hand laid on them afore. Wild as a bunch of antelopes, but a whole lot bigger and stronger. What I had to do was to let them know that I warn't plannin' to eat them alive, and then to learn them that everythin' would be fine if they'd just quit fightin' for their lives and start cooperatin'."

Hy always got that backward-looking drift in his eyes when he started thinking about all those beautiful, brave horses, snorting and squealing and showing the whites of their eyes. After he'd drifted awhile he'd chuckle and say something like, "Some of them ponies was just real determined to learn the hard way. Hard on them, and hard on my poor old bones, too." And then he'd start pointing out all the breaks he'd had and what year the accident had "took place." Gib liked listening to Hy's stories about his days as a rip-roaring wild-horse wrangler, but at the moment he was also concerned about the rip-roaring weather that looked to be headed right in their direction.

At breakfast that morning Hy broke his rule about not talking unless he was spoken to and tried to help Mrs. Thornton convince the boss that he'd better not try to go into Longford. But Mr. Thornton wouldn't listen. He especially refused to listen when Mrs. Thornton tried to remind him what the doctors at Harristown Hospital had told him. "Nonsense," he said sharply. "There's nothing wrong with my health." He went to the window and said, "See, there's not a breath of wind at the moment. And if a storm should blow in during the day, I'll just put up overnight at the hotel."

So Gib harnessed up the bays as usual, and Mr. Thornton went off into the stiffening wind, but without Livy, of course. And sure enough, he didn't get back until two days later. In the meantime it was Gib's eleventh birthday.

Just getting to the big house that second night of the storm hadn't been easy. The blizzard was going full blast by then and the wind-driven snow bit into your cheeks and blinded your eyes. Leaning forward, propped up against the wind, Gib and Hy clung to each other and plunged toward the glowing windows of the big house. Once into the snowshed Hy had set up around the back door, they beat the snow off each other the best they could before they staggered into the kitchen—and into a real birthday party.

It must have been Mrs. Thornton who'd spilled the beans, because Gib hadn't told anybody it was his birthday, not even Hy. For some reason he didn't want anyone to know. He wasn't sure why, although it might have been because it seemed like he wouldn't care so much when nobody mentioned his birthday if the reason was that they just didn't know about it. But Mrs. Thornton must have found out somehow.

Not that a nothing birthday would have been all that much different from the way it had been at Lovell

House. Except that Miss Mooney always kept track of birthdays and asked everyone to be extra nice to the birthday person all day long, as a kind of gift. Often as not, that was all the gift you got. But that night when Gib, half frozen and still pretty well coated with snowflakes, pushed open the kitchen door, the first thing he saw was the crepe-paper decorations and the Thorntons' good china on the table.

There were presents, too. Miss Hooper gave Gib a fancy leather jacket she'd cut down from a man-sized one she'd inherited from a dead uncle. And Mrs. Thornton gave him a new book, a copy of Jack London's *Call of the Wild*. Hy had made him a bootjack, and even Livy had a present for him, a cardboard bookmark on which she had painted a picture of a horse's head. A beautiful head with flaring nostrils, wild, white-rimmed eyes, and a black mane that flowed out right to the edge of the cardboard. And down at one end of the table was a big chocolate birthday cake that turned out to be Mrs. Perry's present.

Everybody talked and talked that night, mostly about old times when the Rocking M Merrills had owned three thousand acres and run their herds on a lot more land besides. And in between the olden-days stories they stopped to listen to the raging wind and talk about the weather. It must have been talking about the blizzard that made Mrs. Perry bring up the subject of the awful storm they'd had a while back—"when old Jebidiah Bean sent that boy out into the cold without his mittens and—"

"Don't!" Livy cried, and when they all looked at her she had her hands over her ears and a tragic expression on her face. "Can't you talk about something more cheerful?" she said.

Mrs. Thornton looked puzzled. "Why, of course we can, dear," she said. "But I didn't know you felt so strongly about it. As I recall, you talked about it a great deal last winter." Livy only ducked her head and, without looking at Gib, said, "That was because I didn't know then how—how sad it was."

When Gib realized what Livy was doing, he thought it was like she wanted to give him another present, besides the bookmark, by keeping anyone from talking about something that would make him feel bad. But when he tried to give her a look that said he understood, she only tossed her head and looked away. And later, when he tried to thank her for the bookmark, she did the same thing.

Lying in bed that night in Hy's loft, under five or six extra blankets, Gib watched Bobby eating birthday cake crumbs, listened to the muted roar of the snow-choked wind, and thought about the birthday party.

The day, in a lot of ways, had been just about the best one of his whole life. The chicken-and-dumplings supper, the chocolate cake that had been made especially for him, and the presents were very much like one of his old hope dreams come to life. Only better. Back then, he never would have been able to even make a dream picture of anything quite so good as that cake. What he'd told

179

everybody as he and Hy were getting ready to head out through the storm was the absolute truth, for sure and certain—that it had been the very best birthday he'd ever had.

But birthdays were one thing, and girls were something else again. Where girls were concerned, at least where Livy Thornton was concerned, there didn't seem to be anything you could call "for sure and certain." It seemed to Gib that just when you thought you had a girl figured and pretty much knew where she was going to head next, she shied off in some other direction entirely.

Thinking about Livy always seemed to bring up problems that, unlike long division and fractions, didn't have any one right answer. Problems without any right answer had always given Gib an uneasy feeling, but as his cold feet warmed up and his thoughts began to drift toward sleep, he came up with a comforting answer. The answer was that not being able to understand girls wasn't really his fault.

After having lived so long at Lovell House, where even laying eyes on a girl was a rare event, it wasn't surprising if the first one he really got acquainted with turned out to be pretty mysterious.

CHAPTER
27

That night, the night of the big blizzard and birthday party, Gib had gone to sleep thinking about how changeable females could be, and a few hours later, when the raging storm wakened him, he found himself thinking about other puzzling changes. Like, for instance, how much everything changed when Mr. Thornton was away from home.

Anytime the rest of them, Gib and Hy and any of the women, were in the kitchen together, things were very different than when Mr. Thornton was there too. Gib wondered if Mr. Thornton had always been so stern and silent and busy with his newspapers, or if having Gib there was what made him act that way. But if he really hated having Gib around, why had he come to Lovell House and signed the papers to take him out of the orphanage?

Perhaps the hatred had come later, after Gib had arrived at the Rocking M. But what had he done to cause it? Unfortunately, it wasn't the kind of thing you could go around asking about. Mrs. Thornton would know the answer, of course, but asking her was out of the question.

"Mrs. Thornton," he imagined himself saying, "could you tell me why your husband hates me?" Not likely. And asking Livy . . . ? Probably not, unless she happened to be in a question-answering frame of mind. Gib went back to sleep wondering how you could tell if a girl was in a question-answering frame of mind. He would, he decided, keep his eyes open and try to find out, and if the opportunity arose, he would ask Livy to tell him why her father hated him.

But the opportunity didn't arise right away. Christmas came and went without much change in Gib's life. The Thorntons had two Christmas dinners, one in the kitchen, as usual, and one in the dining room with a bunch of banking friends. Gib thought the kitchen dinner with its roast chickens and pumpkin pies was fine enough to suit anybody, but Livy had insisted on telling him what the menu would be for the company dinner and sneaking him into the dining room just before the guests arrived so he could see how grand the table looked with its china and crystal and silver candlesticks. Gib was impressed all right, and just a little bit envious. After all, eating *was* one of his favorite occupations.

But when the guests began to arrive he was too busy to care about it. And when all the barn visitors, nine extra horses that day, were unharnessed or unsaddled, rubbed down, fed, and watered and Gib and Hy stood in the central corridor, looking at the almost full rows of stalls, they grinned at each other.

"I guess it almost looks like the old days, huh?" Gib asked.

Hy laughed and agreed. "Mighty close," he said.

"Looks good," Gib said, and Hy agreed with that too. After Hy went back to his cabin Gib stayed in the barn a while longer, getting acquainted with each of the visitors and then spending some time with Lightning and Silky so they wouldn't feel left out. It was a real good Christmas afternoon.

Miss Hooper's Rocking M Institute of Higher Learning went right on operating through January and February. And even during an early thaw in March, Livy went on studying at home, which, according to Miss Hooper, wasn't how it had been in other years. In fact, she complained about it from time to time. About how hard being a teacher was and how she was getting to be too old for the job.

One day when Livy and Gib had just had a long argument about President Taft, Miss Hooper really got fed up. Livy said she would have voted for Taft if she'd been old enough, and Gib started quoting an article he'd read about some of the dumb things Taft had done and how he had to have a special bathtub built when he moved into the White House because he was too fat to fit in a regular one. When Livy wound up not speaking to Gib again, Miss Hooper threw up her hands.

"I give up," Miss Hooper said with a fierce frown. "I give up on both of you. And you, missy," she said to Livy, "weather's not been too bad. Thought you'd be back full-time at Longford School by now. Don't you miss seeing all your school friends?"

Livy shrugged and said she got to see all the ones she liked when she spent weekends in town at Alicia's. "Besides," she said, smiling the too-sweet smile she sometimes used to get forgiven for being particularly hardheaded, "you're a much better teacher."

"Don't use your wiles on me, Miss Thornton," Miss Hooper said. "I don't think my teaching has anything to do with it. What I think is that you just like being around our friend Gib here."

Gib wasn't pleased. It was clear that Miss Hooper was teasing Livy. Trying to get a rise out of her. And he didn't appreciate being part of the teasing. But Livy surprised Miss Hooper—and Gib too. Instead of getting mad and saying how wrong Miss Hooper was, Livy just shrugged and said, "That's right. I like arguing with Gib. No one at Longford School is nearly as much fun to argue with." Then she went back to not speaking, to anybody this time, and Gib went back to wishing that girls weren't so hard to understand.

So Gib continued to be a part of the lessons in the library, at least when no outdoors work needed to be done. During spells of better weather he took some time off in the middle of the day to exercise Silky. And now and then he and Hy, who was riding Lightning again nowadays, took both the horses out onto the prairie.

Those early spring rides with Hy were real workouts for Gib and Silky. Hy would locate a herd of Herefords, mostly cows and calves belonging to the Lazy L, a spread that included a lot of the land that had once belonged to the Rocking M. And then there would be a different kind of school, a stock-handling school with lessons in cutting and roping. Both Gib and Silky had a lot to learn.

With her quick starts and fantastic speed Silky could overtake a calf in no time, but when it came to cutting him out of the herd and heading him in the right direction, Lightning could beat her all to pieces. And as for roping, even though Gib had been doing some extra practicing in the barn, he still had a ways to go. Watching Hy snake out his lasso and catch a steer by his front feet, Gib wondered if he'd ever get the hang of it.

It did occur to Gib now and then to wonder why Hy was bothering to teach him how to be a ranch hand. If the Rocking M were still running cattle, there'd be a reason for it, but as it was . . .

They were on their way back to the barn one day when he asked Hy about it. Hy nodded and grinned, but they'd reached the gate by then, and Hy pulled up to watch how well Silky lined herself up so Gib could lean down and reach the latch. It wasn't until they were through the gate and riding side by side again that Hy said, "Cain't say as

I blame you for askin' about that, seein' as how being a crackerjack stock handler don't cut much ice on a spread that's down to one old milk cow and a bunch of chickens."

They both laughed, but Hy's wrinkled face sobered down in a hurry. "Don't exactly know why I'm pestering you with all this cowhand stuff 'ceptin' it seems to me it's still a mighty useful thing to know. You gettin' tired of it?"

Gib quickly said, "Oh no, I'm not tired of it. I won't be tired of it until—" He grinned. "Until I'm the best cowhand in the whole world."

CHAPTER

28

Livy went right on studying at home until the snow had melted and the bare leafless trees began to show soft green nubs where leaves would soon be sprouting. Gib was still studying in the library, too, even though he hadn't been able to spend as much time there since work had begun in the greenhouse.

He and Hy were planting the sprouting beds so all kinds of vegetables would be up and ready for transplanting as soon as the danger of frost had passed. According to Hy, the greenhouse was mostly Mrs. Perry's idea. Besides being a great cook, Mrs. Perry was practically famous for the blue ribbons her vegetables always won at the county fair. *"Her* vegetables," Hy snorted sarcastically. "Well, they're her blue ribbons, I reckon, but look who has to do the work."

"I'm looking," Gib said, just barely managing to keep a straight face, because Hy was sitting at the end of a row of tomato plants at the time, and had been for an hour or so. As a matter of fact, Hy spent most of the day sitting around grumbling about how disgraceful it was for a top-notch wrangler to wind up scratching in the dirt like a dangbusted gopher, and in the meantime Gib did most of the scratching.

But it was easy work actually, and Gib didn't mind it so long as it left him time to keep up with other things. Like ancient Rome, for instance. It was a test on the Roman Empire that he and Livy were taking one day in late April, when Mr. Thornton came home early and unexpectedly.

It was very quiet in the library. Miss Hooper was reading a book and Gib and Livy were bent over their essays when the library door opened and Mr. Thornton came in. Gib looked up, surprised and shocked. Mr. Thornton came home early now and then when he wasn't feeling well, but he'd never before arrived without the warning clop of hooves and jangle of harness as Caesar and Comet came down the long driveway to the house.

"Well, well. Hard at work, I see," Mr. Thornton said to no one in particular as he took off his overcoat and hung it on the back of a chair.

"Yes, indeed," Miss Hooper said, looking almost as surprised as Gib was feeling. "Finishing up an essay test." She turned then and looked out the window at the hitching rack. "How did you . . . ?"

Mr. Thornton's gray beard split open on his thin smile. "No, not in the buggy," he said. "Mr. Appleton was taking a trial run in a new Model T Ford. Dropped me off out by the gate."

"A Model T?" Livy asked quickly. "Alicia says her folks might be getting a Model T."

"Is that so," Mr. Thornton said. "Well, it's an amazing machine for the price. And a much more comfortable ride than that outdated old Packard Appleton's been trying to sell me. Quieter, too." He turned to Miss Hooper and asked, "Did you hear anything? A car motor out on the road?"

Miss Hooper shook her head. "Not a thing," she said. "But then I wasn't listening for a motorcar. Not after what happened the last time one paid us a visit."

Of course, Miss Hooper was talking about how the team had spooked and run over Hy, but Mr. Thornton only shrugged. "Nonsense," he said. "Can't afford to go on living in the nineteenth century just because of an accident caused by a couple of poorly trained horses. Besides, Caesar and Comet are getting quite used to the sounds of progress. Mr. Appleton's had one of his men working on them while I'm at the bank every day. Getting them used to being around all kinds of motors."

Mr. Thornton walked right past Gib's end of the table and over to the window. "Edgar will stop by shortly to take me back to town," he said over his shoulder. "I told him to come right on down the drive."

Gib had been trying to catch Miss Hooper's eye, hoping to make his face ask, "What now? Am I in trouble or not?" When he finally did, Miss Hooper seemed to think not; at least she frowned back in the phony fierce way that said that as far as she was concerned, the whole thing was pretty amusing. But Livy's face was harder to read. Right at first, when her father suddenly appeared in the library, she'd only shrugged and looked bored, but now, as she went on staring at his back, her eyes began to widen excitedly.

"Papa," she said in a whispery voice, "are we going to get a Model T?"

Mr. Thornton turned back from the window. "I'm thinking about it, Olivia," he said. "I'm giving the matter some serious thought." He smiled again, and on his way to the door he patted Livy's head before he picked up his overcoat and went out.

When the library door swung shut Gib wiped his forehead, and said, "Whew!"

But Livy only laughed. "I told you he knew," she said. "I told you he knew Miss Hooper was teaching you too."

Miss Hooper nodded. "He knew," she agreed. She picked up the tests, first Livy's and then Gib's. "I think we'll call it a day, however. Don't suppose we can expect ancient Rome to compete with a brand-new motorcar." Livy immediately ran out of the room, and after Miss Hooper told Gib the pages he should read that night, she went out, too.

Gib went on sitting at the library table for a few minutes longer, sorting out an uncomfortable mixture of feelings. Relief was there. Relief that Mr. Thornton hadn't objected to his being there, or at least hadn't made a scene, shouting and ordering him out of the room. But in a mysterious way what *had* happened seemed even worse.

He was still sitting there trying to figure out what Mr. Thornton had done and hadn't done, and why it mattered so much, when he heard voices on the front veranda. Lots of voices. Mr. Thornton's first, and then his wife's, and Miss Hooper's, and, a few seconds later, Mrs. Perry's too. Next there was a clatter of rapid footsteps as Livy ran down the veranda steps and her excited voice saying, "He's coming. I can hear it. Can't you?" Gib got up slowly and went to the window just as a big, shiny motorcar roared and bounced its way down the drive.

The Model T was longer than a big buckboard. It had a high windshield made of glass, with a lantern on each side, front and back seats, and a leathery black roof to keep off the rain and sun. Mr. Appleton, a fattish man with a sporty motoring cap on his bald, dome-shaped head, drove right up to the hitching rack. The moment he climbed down, Livy was all over the Model T, sitting in one seat and then the other, and jabbering away like an excited chipmunk.

Gib went on watching while the Thorntons talked to Mr. Appleton and then while Mr. Appleton helped get Mrs. Thornton's chair down the steps and over to the Model T. But when they were all gathered around the gleaming motorcar, talking and staring and pointing, Gib suddenly didn't want to watch anymore.

It was quiet in the barn. Silky looked up and nickered

softly as he entered her stall. He let her rub her soft nose against his cheek, and then he stretched his arms up around the arching curve of her neck. For a while he rested his face against her neck and then, using the edge of the feed trough as a mounting block, he climbed up onto her back. She looked back questioningly for a moment, as if asking if they were going somewhere, and then went back to nuzzling around in her feed bucket, looking for the last crumbs of oats. Tucking his feet up behind him, Gib stretched out on his stomach with his head on his arms. Lying there on the mare's strong, warm back, it wasn't too hard to keep his mind there with her. With Silky, there in the barn at first and then, in his imagination, out on the prairie, letting her outrun the wind.

It must have been almost an hour later when he heard the distant hiccups of a starting motor, and then a steady roar that faded slowly away down the drive and out onto the road to Longford.

"Hey," he told Silky, "must be almost milking time." Sliding down off her back, he was reaching over to unlatch the gate when she nickered and shoved him gently with her nose—and suddenly, for no reason at all, he was crying. Crying like an Infant Room baby. Burying his face against the mare's soft neck, he clenched his teeth until the tears stopped and the ache in his throat died away. When he finally raised his head, Silky was looking at him curiously.

"Yeah," he told her. "Pretty silly, huh?" Giving her a

last pat, he whispered against her tear-wet neck, "Nothing to cry about, is there? It's a whole lot better than Mr. Bean's, anyway."

Halfway across the barnyard he ran into Hy carrying the milking pail. It was time to get back to work.

CHAPTER

29

It was right after the Thorntons bought the Model T that Livy started going back to Longford School, riding in again with her father every morning. Except that now she was riding in a brand-new motorcar instead of a buggy. She had some new clothes too, a motoring hat with a long, thin scarf to tie under her chin to keep the hat from flying away, and a long coat that she called a duster.

And on the east side of the house, as far away from the barn as possible, a Longford construction company was putting up a fancy new building. When Gib told Hy that the new building was called a garage and that it was where the Model T would be parked, Hy scowled and grunted, "Garage, huh. Well, leastways it's a good thing he's not goin' to try to keep it here in the barn with the horses. If he did that, I'd have to shoot."

"Shoot?" Gib asked uneasily. "Who'd you shoot, Hy?"

Hy grinned and pretended to draw a six-shooter. "I'd have to shoot the dadburned thing right between the headlights."

Gib went on studying with Miss Hooper, but not quite as often, since spring was such a busy time for him, with the hayfield and Mrs. Perry's kitchen garden to be plowed and planted. But before the plowing could start, Hy had to teach Gib about how to handle the stubborn old mules, and how to steer them with the reins around his shoulders so his hands would be free to hold the plow. Hy seemed to know all about it, even though he liked to say that plows were for good-for-nothin' range-spoilin' sodbusters, and any real stockman hated the sight of them.

"How come a real stockman like you knows how to plow, then?" Gib asked him when Hy was showing him how to sight across the field to keep the furrow going in a straight line.

Hy grunted disgustedly. "A man learns how to do what he has to do," he growled, "just like you're doing, Gibby Whittaker."

It didn't take Gib long, however, to discover that Hy sure enough meant it when he said he hated the sight of a plow. Leastways he hated it enough to find a lot of other things he absolutely had to tend to while Gib did most of the plowing. Of course, you did need good strong legs to plow all day, and Hy's bum leg was still giving him quite a bit of trouble.

But when the planting was finished there was a little

more time for Gib to catch up on some of the things he'd missed out on. School subjects like the Revolutionary War, and Milton's *Paradise Lost*. Not to mention roping practice and working with Black Silk.

As soon as there was time, and good weather, Gib went back to working Silky in the corral whenever he got a chance. And when June came and Longford School was out for summer vacation, Livy started watching the training from the roof again. Gib kept telling himself that someday he was going to ask her why she was watching, without really believing that he ever would.

Even though it was a school vacation month, Gib went on studying nights in the cabin and meeting with Miss Hooper now and then. And it was on one of those now-and-then afternoons, when he'd been parsing sentences, that Livy came in. She said her mother had sent her to get Miss Hooper, but after Miss Hooper left, Livy sat down at the table and began to ask Gib questions about what he was doing. When he showed her the parsed sentences, she said, "Oh yes, I learned how to do that a long time ago. Look." She pointed to the sentence Gib was working on. "That's not right. That part is a prepositional phrase."

Gib didn't think so, but he didn't argue because right at the moment he had something else on his mind. Something like asking a few questions his own self. "That right?" he said, shutting his notebook. "I'll fix it later. But look here, unless you're specially in the mood for parsing sentences, I'd like to change the subject.

There's something else I've been thinking to ask you about for quite a spell."

Livy blinked and swallowed. "About what?" she said suspiciously, as if she felt a lot easier with questions that she'd had the choosing of. "What do you want to know about?"

"I'd like to know why you watch me and Black Silk so much. You know, from up there on the roof?" He grinned. "I thought you said you hated . . ." He stopped then on purpose, waiting to see how she would finish the sentence.

Livy stared at him for a long moment. Wide-eyed at first and then with her lips curling in a teasing smile, the way she always did when she wanted to rile somebody. "Oh, you mean what I said that day in the barn about hating you?" she asked.

"Um," he said, "yeah, I guess you said that too. But I meant when you said you hated Black Silk. Seems kind of strange, you spending all that time watching something you hate so much."

Livy's eyes blazed. "You quit grinning at me like that, Gibson Whittaker," she said between anger-thinned lips. "You don't know what you're talking about. You just don't know. . . . You just don't know anything." Suddenly the anger seemed to have burned itself out, and what was left looked like the beginning of tears.

"Hey, I'm sorry," Gib said hastily. "I'm really sorry, Livy. You don't have to tell me. . . ."

But suddenly she tossed her head, narrowed her eyes,

and said, "All right, I *will* tell you. I promised I wouldn't tell you anything, but I will tell that much. About Black Silk and why I said I hated her, anyway." She took a deep breath. "I guess you know that she's the reason my mother can't walk. Because Black Silk threw my mother and broke her back and almost killed her. Did you know that?"

Gib nodded. "I heard that. But the way I heard it was that she didn't mean to throw your mother. She just reared up because something scared her and she slipped and fell over backward. What I think . . ." Gib paused, remembering how Silky had greeted Mrs. Thornton that day when she came out to the corral. "What I think is that Silky really likes your mother a lot and she'd never mean to—"

"All right! All right!" Livy interrupted. "I don't care about that. I don't care about what she meant to do. That's not the reason I hate her, anyway. The reason I hate her is because they fight about her. My mother and father. Way back when I was only four or five years old, I used to hear them fighting about Black Silk. About what to do with her."

"What to do with her?"

"Yes. My father wanted to shoot her, I guess, right at first, but even after he'd promised he wouldn't do that, he wanted to sell her. He said no one was riding her anymore and no one ever would, and he couldn't bear to look at her, and they ought to get rid of her. And my mom said that Hy would ride her, and that if my father got rid of Black Silk, she would leave too. I heard them fighting and fighting and I—I thought it was Black Silk's fault. I guess I thought if it wasn't for that stupid horse everything would be all right again."

Gib understood then. At least he understood a lot more than he had. Livy had turned away so he couldn't see her face, but there was something about the way she was holding her head that made him feel real sorry that he'd brought it up. "I'm sorry," he said. "I shouldn't have asked you about it."

She nodded, still looking away. They sat that way for a long time before she sighed and turned around. "I didn't answer your question, did I?"

"My question?" Gib had almost forgotten what he'd asked.

"About why I watch you and Black Silk."

"Well, maybe you didn't," Gib said. "But that's all right. I don't really want to know anymore."

"I don't know why I do," she said. "I don't . . ." She stopped talking then and her eyes went distant and dreamy. "Except that when I watch her it's like . . . I don't know what, except it's like looking at all kinds of beautiful things, like paintings or sunsets, only better, because she is so proud and alive and—" She broke off, looking embarrassed. Then she laughed and shrugged. "I don't know why. It just makes me feel . . ." Putting one hand on her chest, she sighed deeply. "It just makes me feel something in here."

Gib knew exactly what she meant. Did he ever know.

He didn't know how to tell her and he didn't think it would be a good idea to try, but he was pretty sure it meant she had the same kinds of feelings about horses that he had. Feelings like he had, and Livy's mother had, and probably the way his own mother had felt, too. But all he did was nod some more and try to make his face say something helpful.

After a while Livy jumped up and said, "Oh, I'd better go and let you finish your sentences." She sounded like her normal self again as she added, "You'd better fix that prepositional phrase."

At the door she stopped, looked back, and said, "I hated you for the very same reason." Then she went out and slammed the door shut behind her.

CHAPTER

30

Right at first Gib didn't know what to think. He didn't have any idea what Livy was talking about when she said she'd "hated him for the very same reason." It wasn't until he was finishing the milking that evening that it finally dawned on him what that reason might have been. What she must have meant was she hated him because her parents fought about him, just like they fought about Black Silk. It was so obvious once he figured it out, he wondered why he hadn't known immediately. That evening at supper he made a point of noticing things that proved that he'd guessed right.

Like how Mr. Thornton was always silent and unsmiling, busying himself with a newspaper, not speaking much to anybody, and never to Gib. Of course, Mrs. Thornton didn't talk to Gib much, either, but she did ask him how many eggs he'd found that day and, like always, whenever she caught his eye she smiled at him. So he supposed that meant he'd been right in guessing that Mr. Thornton wanted to get rid of him and Mrs. Thornton didn't. Just like Black Silk. The only thing was, in his case, he couldn't figure out why.

It wasn't too hard to see why Mrs. Thornton wanted him to stay. She wanted him to go right on exercising and caring for Black Silk. That wasn't hard to understand. And the mare was probably the reason that Mr. Thornton wanted to get rid of him. Because if Gib wasn't there to take care of her, he'd have a better reason to insist on selling her. But the hard part to figure was why Mr. Thornton had gone to all the trouble to go to Lovell House to get Gib and bring him home, if he hated having him around so much.

For a while he considered the notion that Mr. Thornton had agreed to take Gib on and then something had changed his mind. Like maybe he thought Gib wasn't doing a good job. But he couldn't really believe that was it. Maybe he hadn't done as good a job as a full-grown man could do, but he'd certainly worked awfully hard and the other people at the Rocking M, Hy and Mrs. Thornton and Miss Hooper and even Mrs. Perry, were always saying what a good hard worker he was.

So why had Livy's parents fought about him? The more he thought about it, the more he felt he just had to find out. He thought of asking Hy, but he was pretty sure Hy wouldn't answer. He'd quit answering any question that had anything to do with the Thorntons. And he hated to try to ask Livy again, since she'd gotten so upset about it before. But maybe he'd just have to. He'd have to get up the nerve to ask Livy why her father wanted to get rid of him. He'd do it, he promised himself, the next time he got a chance to talk to her alone. But then, when he started having a lot of good chances, he kept putting it off.

The chances to talk happened because not long after she'd told Gib how she felt when she watched Black Silk, Livy started watching a lot more, and from not so far away. It began one afternoon when Gib was saddling the mare for their afternoon workout.

He had just finished cinching up the girth and was fixing to lead the mare out of the barn when he realized that Livy was there again, just outside the stall door, exactly where she'd been more than a year ago when she'd yelled that she hated Black Silk and Gib too. But now there was a different expression on her face, and it didn't look much like hate.

"Hello," she said as soon as Gib turned around. "How did you get the bridle on her head? I watched you put the saddle on, but you'd already finished with the bridle when I came in."

So Gib took Black Silk's bridle off and put it back on again while Livy watched and asked questions. "What if she bites you?" she wanted to know. "What if she bites when you hold the bit up there to her mouth that way?"

Gib laughed. "Well, if she bit me, I reckon I'd be pretty sorry," he said. "But she's not going to. Silky's real sweet about taking the bit. You don't even have to stick your finger in her mouth, the way you do with Lightning sometimes."

"You stick your finger in his mouth?" Livy sounded horrified.

"Sure do. Like this." Gib pulled Silky around and lifted up one side of her lip so Livy could see how horses' grazing teeth end before their chewing teeth begin. "See this gap right here where there's no teeth? You just stick your finger in here and . . ."

He stopped then to swallow a grin. Livy was staring wide-eyed, looking horrified and fascinated at the same time. "Ooh," she squealed. "Ooh, ooh." But then, noticing the expression on Gib's face, she calmed down and said, "Ugh, that's disgusting." And as Gib opened the stall and started to lead Silky out, Livy backed up hastily and then ran out of the barn.

But she kept coming back. Almost every weekday in the early afternoon, about the time Gib finished with his other chores and before it was time for Mr. Thornton's return from Longford, Livy would suddenly show up in the barn. She'd watch and ask questions while Gib saddled up, and when he led the mare out, Livy would run ahead to open the corral gate. After that she would climb up on the fence and sit there watching and asking questions.

Right at first she only watched from a safe distance, but one day when Gib was unsaddling, Livy opened the stall door and stepped inside. Gib went on with what he was doing, pretending he didn't notice, until Livy asked in a breathy whisper, "Could I touch her? Would she let me touch her?"

"Sure," Gib said. "Just reach out slow like. Horses don't like sudden things. Okay?"

"Yes," Livy breathed, being so careful she even nodded slowly. "Slowly." So then Gib untied Silky's reins and turned her head around, and as the mare stretched out her neck and sniffed curiously, Livy reached out and touched the velvety nose. Touched and rubbed slowly and gently—but with an expression on her face that looked to Gib like some kind of explosion was happening inside her head.

Afterward, when Silky and Lightning had been fed, Livy said it had been the most exciting moment of her whole life, and when Gib laughed she said angrily, "It was. I mean it. Don't you remember? Wasn't it the most exciting moment of your life the first time you ever touched a horse?" And when Gib said he didn't think he could remember back that far, she suddenly sighed and said, "You're lucky. You're so lucky."

But when Gib laughed and said, "Lucky? I'm lucky?" she shrugged, "You know what I mean. You're lucky you've been with horses all your life that way, instead of—instead of being taught terrible things about them."

"Taught?" Gib asked, and she nodded.

"My father. My father talks about horses like they were worse than rattlesnakes. He always has. He hates horses. That's why I thought I hated them, I guess."

They were standing outside Silky's stall at the time,

watching as she picked up each mouthful of hay, shook it, and then chewed contentedly, occasionally turning her head to see if they were still there. Watching horses eat had always given Gib a contented feeling, but now suddenly the contentment was invaded by the sudden remembrance of the promise he'd made himself.

"Livy," he said, "he hates me too, doesn't he? Why does your father hate me?"

She didn't answer right away. Instead she only frowned and shook her head. After a minute she sighed and said, "He doesn't hate you. I don't think he hates you." But she didn't sound very certain.

"Well, okay," Gib said. "But he doesn't like my being here, does he? He wishes I didn't have to be here."

Livy nodded reluctantly. But then suddenly she set her jaw. "I can't tell you anything more," she said, "because I promised. We had to promise things before he would go to get you out of the orphanage. And I had to promise and promise I wouldn't tell you about—about what I promised. But you know what? I don't think Miss Hooper promised anything." Jumping to her feet, she grabbed Gib's sleeve and pulled him toward the house. "Come on," she said. "Let's find Miss Hooper."

CHAPTER

31

They found Miss Hooper on the veranda. She was sitting on the porch swing drinking lemonade and reading a book and when they started up the stairs, she kind of winced and then frowned. "Hello, hello," she said warily. "What have we here? Why do I have the feeling I'm witnessing a twentieth-century version of the children's crusade?"

Gib couldn't help smiling, but Livy just marched on up the stairs and down the veranda. When she was right in front of Miss Hooper she put her hands on her hips and demanded, "You've got to tell Gib the truth, Miss Hooper. The truth about why he's here and why my parents fought about it. I had to promise I wouldn't tell him anything about it, but he needs to know. Don't you, Gib?"

Miss Hooper thought for a moment before she carefully moved her bookmark and closed her book. "Is that right, Gibson?" she asked. "And what is it exactly that you want to ask me?"

Gib grinned ruefully. "That's just it, Miss Hooper," he said. "I don't rightly know. Except I guess I just need to find out why I feel like I don't belong here. Like my being here is why everyone is so—so angry."

"Would you like to live somewhere else, Gibson?" Miss Hooper's face looked strangely blank, without even its usual sarcastic frown.

Gib shook his head quickly. "No," he said. "I wouldn't. Not unless—that is, not unless there's no other way to . . ." He paused. "Not unless there's no other way to calm things down." He shrugged and smiled. "Besides, I don't have anyplace else to go."

They were both staring at him. "See!" Livy almost shouted at Miss Hooper. "See how he said that. That's the way he is about everything."

"What way is that, child?" Miss Hooper asked.

Livy shrugged angrily. "I don't know. Calm, I guess. He's just so calm and cheerful about *everything*." She threw up her hands. "It drives me crazy."

Miss Hooper frowned at Gib and said, "Pretty serious accusation, Gibson. Do you plead guilty to being calm and cheerful?" One corner of Gib's mouth began to turn up, but Livy ignored him and went on, "Tell him, Miss Hooper. Tell him what my mother wanted to do after his mother died and—" She stopped then and clenched her lips for a second, and when she opened them she said, "If you don't, I'm going to. Even if I go straight to hell for it.

If you don't tell him, I'm going to break a promise I made on the Bible and tell him myself."

"And no doubt make a complete muddle of it," Miss Hooper said. "All right, I'll tell him what I know, but on one condition. I want you out of it. If you'll go into the kitchen and make us up another pitcher of lemonade, I promise to explain everything. As far as it's explainable, anyway."

Right at first Livy stomped her foot and said no, she wouldn't go, but when Miss Hooper just sat there staring at her she finally flounced away and marched off toward the kitchen door.

Miss Hooper sighed and told Gib to pull up a chair, and when he was sitting she started in.

"The quarrel between Henry and Julia started soon after your mother died. At least the part of it that concerned you. Actually it had started long before that. Disagreements over the selling of her parents' land, and then Julia's accident and the arguments about the fate of her mare." She paused, and Gib nodded.

"I've heard about that."

"But then when your mother died, Julia told Henry that she wanted to adopt you."

"Adopt me?" A strange, hot lump was rising in Gib's throat.

"Yes. But Henry wouldn't hear of it."

"Why?" Gib could manage only a whisper around the lump in his throat. "Why wouldn't he . . . Why did he hate me?"

"No, child, he didn't hate you. I'm not sure if he'd ever actually seen you at that time, although I know Julia had seen you several times when you were an infant." She paused again, nodding thoughtfully. "In fact," she finally went on, "to be fair to Henry, he had some fairly sensible reasons for the stand he took. You weren't yet recovered from a very close call with typhoid yourself and there was some doubt if you would ever be quite well again, physically and mentally too. And of course Julia was an invalid herself by then. Then Julia became ill—not typhoid, as it turned out, but probably quite a severe case of influenza. And while she was still in the hospital in Harristown you had recovered enough to be sent to the orphanage. Henry was a member of a group of city officials who made the decision. By the time Julia was well again you had been at the orphanage for some time, and Julia eventually accepted the situation. For a time she believed that leaving you at Lovell House couldn't be any worse than bringing you up in a home where there was so much disagreement and unhappiness." Miss Hooper paused and sipped her lemonade before she went on. "At least that was how she was feeling until the furor over the Bean case."

"The Bean case? Oh, you mean about Georgie Olson?" Gib whispered.

"Yes indeed. Folks around here knew old Bean's reputation, and there was a great deal of anger over the fact that the orphanage would indenture another child to that cruel old man. Julia was particularly upset. She wrote to

Lovell House to know if you were still there and when she found you were, she began to press for adoption again. But Henry wouldn't hear of it. His point was that there was no telling what all those years in an institution might have done to you emotionally, and what diseases you might have been exposed to."

Miss Hooper shrugged and circled her right hand in an "on and on forever" gesture. "So the argument went on for months, and then Hy's broken leg tipped the scale. Henry was faced with hiring a full-time salaried replacement or, as we all pointed out to him—yes, Julia, Hy, and even I myself were involved in the argument at that time—taking on an indentured orphan."

Suddenly Gib knew what Hy had meant when he'd said his broken leg had turned out to be a "bargaining chip." He was still thinking about how Hy's poor old broken leg had helped Gib Whittaker when he realized Miss Hooper was still talking.

"But as always, Henry had the last word," she was saying. "Apparently promises were demanded of Julia and Olivia, and I think of Hy too, before Henry agreed to go to Lovell House and sign the papers. But only such papers that would be necessary to bring you to the Rocking M as hired help. And he insisted that you were to be treated as such."

There was a long silence before Gib swallowed hard, tried to speak, and then tried again. "Are they still fighting about—about what to do with me?"

Miss Hooper looked at him for a long time, and there

was a different kind of frown on her face. An angry frown, but one that somehow made it clear that the anger wasn't meant for Gib Whittaker.

"Not exactly fighting," she said. "Not recently, at least. Perhaps you've noticed that Henry hasn't been too well recently. He's had other things to worry about."

"He doesn't ever seem to see me," Gib said.

Miss Hooper made a snorting noise. "Well, don't let that worry you, child. There's a whole world of important things that Henry Thornton manages not to see. And don't blame yourself, Gibson Whittaker. You're only one of a hundred things Henry and Julia have found to torment each other about."

CHAPTER

32

No more than a minute after Miss Hooper stopped talking, Livy appeared on the veranda carrying a tray. Watching her make her way toward them, Miss Hooper sighed and said, "Perfect timing." Then she leaned back in the swing and closed her eyes. Livy set the pitcher and glasses down on one of the veranda's little round tables, filled Miss Hooper's glass, and poured two more for herself and Gib before she said, "Well, I guess you know all about that ancient history now, so let's talk about something more cheerful." And then she began to tell about a fight two fifth-grade boys had had on the front steps of Longford School on the last day of school, and how, before it was over, they'd both had black eyes and bloody noses and one of them had a broken front tooth.

When Livy had finished, Miss Hooper opened her eyes and said, "Well, I must say I'm glad you explained you were going to tell us something cheerful, Olivia. Otherwise I might have taken that little tale for a bloody tragedy."

So then Olivia explained that it *was* a cheerful story because Rodney and Alvin were both horrid and it would have been even more cheerful if they'd broken each other's necks.

Miss Hooper sighed again and said, "Oh, I see." Then she waved them away and went back to her book. Gib and Livy headed for the barn, where Gib finished grooming Black Silk and Livy went on talking. At one point she asked if he felt better or worse now that he'd heard everything, and he said he didn't know yet. "Not until I have a chance to think about it some more. Besides," he wanted to know, "how do you know how much I heard?"

"Oh, I heard it, too," Livy said. "I got Mrs. Perry to make the lemonade and then I went into the parlor and—"

"Listened at the window." Gib grinned. "Thought so. I thought I saw something behind the curtains."

But Livy had stopped paying attention. "Shhh," she said, and then Gib heard it too, the distant chug and clank of the Model T. A second later Livy was on her way back to the house and Gib was putting away the grooming tack and heading for the milking barn.

That night at supper Gib watched Henry and Julia Thornton in a different way and thought about what his life would have been like if Mrs. Thornton had won the argument and they had really adopted him right after his mother died. It would have been a true adoption, not a farming out; he would have lived in a big, beautiful house; and there would have been other good things about it. But he knew now that it wouldn't have been very much like his old dream.

That night on his cot in the cabin loft, Gib's mind ran in circles, going back over everything he'd learned that day and trying to decide how he ought to feel about it. It wasn't until Bobby the field mouse showed up, checking out pockets, racing around the bed, and sniffing accusingly at Gib's hands and face that he was able to get his mind to stop whirling long enough to realize that he'd forgotten to bring anything at all for Bobby. But then he remembered seeing a piece of dried-up venison in one of Hy's cupboards, and after he'd been down to get it, both he and Bobby were able to settle down some, Bobby to start the hard work of making a meal out of a strip of tough old venison, and Gib to start drifting uncertainly in the general direction of sleep.

In the days that followed, even though Livy went on spending quite a lot of time in the barn, she and Gib didn't talk much about her father and mother, or about any of Gib's other problems. Instead they talked mostly about horses in general, and Black Silk in particular.

It was becoming more and more obvious that Olivia Thornton, like her mother, loved horses, and that she was absolutely crazy about Black Silk. She had a lot to learn, however, and for the first time ever, she was willing to listen to Gib's opinions and advice without disagreeing with everything he said. At least not very often.

Gib taught her the right way to use the brush and currycomb and hoof pick, and how to take care of a sweated-up horse after a hard workout. How to saddle and bridle too, and keep your tack clean and neat. Most of it was what he'd learned from Hy, and it was stuff that Hy could have taught Olivia years ago if she'd known that she wanted to learn.

Years ago—but perhaps not now. Neither Gib nor Livy knew how Hy would react if he knew how much time Livy was spending in the barn. At least they didn't until one day in August when they were both in the stall. Livy was braiding Silky's mane while Gib brushed her tail. And suddenly someone said, "Would you look at that." And there Hy was, at the stall door.

Livy got down off the grooming stool and started telling Hy about all the things she had been learning, and for a while he only listened with a disapproving expression on his face. Gib was watching him closely, and it was quite some time before Hy's worried frown wrinkles began to rearrange themselves into a grin.

"Well now, young lady, I can see you've had a mighty fine teacher. I'd give you a job on a spread of mine any day of the week."

He went on to ask Livy questions about the things she'd learned to do, and it wasn't until he was about to leave that he said, "Don't see any harm in what you're doing, Livy, but I can't help thinkin' it would be a good thing if you washed up real good before your father gets home. And maybe put on a dash of that flowery-smelling stuff you ladies wear." And when Livy asked if he meant that she smelled like a horse, he said, "Well, just a bit. Smells right good to me, but we don't know what your father would say. Do we? We surely don't know what your father would say."

They both knew what he meant, and Livy said she'd take his advice about washing up. Hy went on back to his cabin then, but that night after supper he talked to Gib some more about what Livy had been doing.

"It was bound to happen sooner or later," Hy said. "Don't matter what the boss tried to drum into her. Horses are in her blood natural as runnin's in the blood of that black mare. Sooner or later Livy's blood would have found her out." He grinned at Gib. "Your comin' along just hurried things up a little."

Gib said he was sure Hy was right about that. "You could see it plain as day the first time she was up on Silky," he told Hy. "Just the way she looked sitting there."

But now Hy was looking worried again. "You mean you've let her ride the mare?" he asked.

"Not really ride," Gib said. "But she's sat on Silky some while I led her up and down inside the barn. She wants to go out in the corral but she's going to ask her mother first."

Hy was shaking his head. "Well, you be sure she does that. Get Miss Julia's say-so. And don't let Livy get ahead of herself. She'll be good with the mare, like as not, but not as good as you were. Nowhere near as good as you were."

Gib felt flattered. Flattered and puzzled. When he asked, though, Hy only said he couldn't rightly put it into words. But after he'd thought awhile he started trying. "There's two things is important with horses," he said finally. "One of them's confidence, and Livy's got bushels of that. But the other one is deeper like. It's what I'd call . . ." He paused, scratching his tumbleweed head. "It's more a kind of—steadiness. Like some people don't feel the need to go thrashin' around proving who they are. Horses feel that steadiness in a person. Settles them right down."

So Gib promised that he wouldn't let Livy get ahead of herself, but at the time he wasn't taking into account the fact that Olivia Thornton was pretty much born ahead of herself. And it wasn't any more than a week later that she set about proving it for good and all.

Gib and Hy were irrigating the vegetable garden that day. The weather had been so hot and dry that some serious irrigating had become necessary, which always meant a lot of extra work. Hard work like digging ditches and moving pipes and hoses from one furrow to another. They had things pretty well under way when they heard Mrs. Perry ringing the bell for the noon meal. They washed up a bit at the standpipe and were heading toward the house when everything began to happen at once.

They were almost to the barnyard when Gib became

aware of the distant sound of a motorcar. And just about then Hy said, "Sounds like the Model T. Did the boss say he'd be home early?"

Gib grinned and shook his head. "You know the boss never says anything to me. Must have come back for something he forgot. Or else he's sick again maybe."

They'd closed the gate and were just coming into the barnyard when the back door of the house opened and Mr. Thornton came down the steps and headed directly for the barn. They were close enough by then to see his face and the tight frown that narrowed his eyes, clenched his lips, and set muscles twitching in his jaw. When he reached the barn door he unlatched it and shouted as it swung open.

"Olivia," Mr. Thornton was yelling. "Olivia! What are you—" He jumped back then, staggering to one side, as from the barn's dimly lit interior there came the thunder of hooves and Black Silk burst out into the barnyard. A saddled and bridled Black Silk, who plunged into the sunlight carrying Livy Thornton on her back. Livy was dressed in trousers and riding astride, and her face glowed with a mixture of excitement and fear. But as Mr. Thornton yelled and lunged to grab the reins, Silky whirled away and danced sideways across the yard, lifting her legs high and floating her long tail like a proud black flag.

For a fraction of a second Gib was too stunned to react, so it was Hy who made the first move. As Silky, confused by Livy's frantic jerks on the reins, whirled and headed across the yard, Hy lurched forward just in time to block the way to the drive and the open road beyond. But when he threw out his arms and yelled, "Whoa. Whoa, baby," the mare's skidding stop only turned into a snorting, sidestepping retreat.

Not meaning any harm, she wasn't. Gib could see that. Just feeling her oats and showing off, but a kind of showing off that was scaring Livy and threatening to dump her on the hard-packed earth of the barnyard. Losing one stirrup and her balance, Livy had dropped the reins, grabbed frantically for the saddle horn, and was slipping farther and farther to one side.

Okay, Silky, that's enough, Gib thought, and he told her so. Told Silky firmly but calmly to stop acting crazy and settle down. And at the sound of his voice the dancing, skittering mare pricked her ears toward him, gave a final little head-tossing celebration, and quieted to a quivering standstill. Gib walked over and picked up the dragging reins.

On the mare's back, Livy clung to the saddle horn, her face flushed with fright, but also with what looked to be a strange sort of triumph.

But her father's face was flushed, too, and he was striding toward them yelling in a way that might have set Silky off again if Hy hadn't cut him off, grabbed his arm, and pulled him to a stop.

So the crisis was over and nobody was hurt, but less than an hour after Livy was safely down on the ground and Black Silk back in her stall, Gib was on his way back to the Lovell House orphanage.

CHAPTER

33

Nothing much had been said between the moment when Mr. Thornton found Livy riding Black Silk and the time, less than an hour later, when the Model T bounced down the driveway carrying Gib, a canvas bag full of his clothing, two saddles, and a silver-studded bridle. Nothing much had been said by Mr. Thornton, at least, or by Gib. Hy had said quite a lot, not that it did any good.

"It warn't the boy's fault," Hy had said over and over again. "He warn't even in the barn this mornin'. Been out in the field with me ever since breakfast."

But Mr. Thornton only glared at Hy, grabbed Gib's arm, and started off around the house toward the Model T. Hy hobbled along behind them still talking and asking questions. "Where you takin' him? Where you goin' to take the boy?"

Mr. Thornton's whole face was tight as a closed fist,

and something twitched in his cheek like the tendons in the face of an angry horse. "Back to where he belongs," he muttered between clenched teeth. "The orphanage. Go get his belongings. We're leaving in ten minutes."

Mr. Thornton pulled Gib around to the front of the house, where the motorcar was parked. "Get in," he said. "Get up there in the backseat." As he disappeared back the way he'd come, he added, "And stay there."

Gib sat in the backseat of the Model T and tried to make sense of what was happening. He'd never been in a motorcar before, but he couldn't even think to be curious. He wasn't, in fact, thinking very clearly about anything, except to wonder if the whole thing was a nightmare and whether he would wake up in a minute and find himself back in the loft in Hy's cabin. But it wasn't a nightmare and in a few minutes, or maybe it was half an hour—time was another thing he was finding it hard to keep track of—Mr. Thornton came back, with Hy and Livy right behind him. Hy was carrying a duffel bag and Livy was yelling at the top of her lungs.

"It wasn't his fault! He didn't have anything to do with it," Livy was yelling. And when her father went on ignoring her, she started yelling something else. "I saddled her myself, and I rode her. And I'm going to go right on riding her, no matter what you say."

That was the first thing anyone said that Mr. Thornton seemed to have heard. Whirling around, he stared at Livy, and then he disappeared again, heading back toward the barn with Livy running behind him. "You can't," Gib heard her yell. "You can't hurt Silky. You promised Mother you wouldn't. You promised."

It was then that Gib started to get down and go after them, but Hy stopped him. "Stay there, Gibby," he said. "Ain't nothin' you can do. And don't worry. He won't hurt the mare none. He's a hard man to figure, the boss is, but he don't break a promise."

So Gib didn't do anything, and in a few minutes Mr. Thornton came back carrying the silver-studded bridle and sidesaddle, as well as the small roping saddle that had been Livy's mother's and that she had given to Gib Whittaker after she'd watched him riding Black Silk.

Throwing all the tack into the backseat, Mr. Thornton cranked up the motor and climbed into the driver's seat. At the last minute, while the motor was choking and heaving to life, Mrs. Perry came out the front door, trotted heavily up to the Model T, and, glaring at Mr. Thornton's back, thrust a good-smelling package into Gib's hands. Then the Model T roared down the drive carrying Gib away from the Rocking M on his way back to where he'd come from—the Lovell House orphanage.

But somehow it all still seemed as unreal as a bad dream. One of those terrible dreams in which awful things keep happening and nothing you do makes it any better, except that you kind of halfway understand that you're only dreaming and that all you have to do is wake up. This time, though, the waking up was only to the certainty that it was not a dream.

It seemed to Gib that it was the good smell of Mrs.

Perry's package that did it. Suddenly there it was—the reality of no more of Mrs. Perry's cooking. And no more of Miss Hooper's friendly frowns, or Hy's honking laugh and head full of old stories about horses and the men who rode them. It was real all right. Gib swallowed hard, and for the next few miles he had to fight against a painful pressure in his throat and a hot flood that threatened his eyes.

They hadn't gone more than a few miles, however, when Mr. Thornton pulled over to the side, stomped on pedals, shoved levers, and just sat there, staring straight ahead. It was on a straight stretch of road several miles from the Rocking M, and Gib's first thought was that he was going to be put out and left all alone on the prairie. But then he noticed that Mr. Thornton was fishing around in a small box that he had pulled from his coat pocket. He found something, put it in his mouth, and then continued to sit stiffly, with both hands clutching the steering wheel. He stayed that way for a long time.

After a while Gib leaned forward until he could see Mr. Thornton's lean, bearded face. His eyes were closed and he seemed to be breathing extra hard. "Mr. Thornton, sir," Gib said at last. "Are you all right?"

The man's head jerked up then, and, turning to look at Gib, he said, "Yes, yes, quite all right." But then he went back to clutching the wheel and breathing heavily. Several minutes later he straightened up, looked around, and then started to push and stomp on things again. But it was then that the motor, which had been chugging away softly, hiccuped violently and died. Moving very slowly, Mr. Thornton started to climb down out of the driver's seat, but Gib said, "I'll do it, sir. I think I can do it."

Cranking up the car was a lot harder than it looked, but with Mr. Thornton calling instructions, Gib finally managed to bring the motor back to life. When he started to climb back up into the rear seat, Mr. Thornton motioned to the seat beside him and said, "Here. Sit here."

They went on then, sitting side by side. But sitting there in the bouncing, rattling motorcar, it occurred to Gib that, what with the motor dying and all, the two of them had just had more of a conversation than they'd had in all the days since Gib arrived at the Rocking M. However, it now seemed the talking was over, and it wasn't until they'd reached the outskirts of Harristown that Gib got up his nerve to say, "Mr. Thornton, sir." And then, "I don't think she'll take me back. Miss Offenbacher has a rule about not letting anyone come back."

Mr. Thornton made a grunting, questioning sound before he nodded and said, "She'll let you stay. I think I can promise you that much."

Gib felt surprised, but not much else. He certainly didn't feel much better. Not that he doubted Mr. Thornton's promise. Hy said that Mr. Thornton didn't break promises, and Gib believed it. It was just that it wasn't too easy to feel good about a promise that he could stay at Lovell House. Gib was still wondering how much Mr. Thornton knew about Miss Offenbacher and her rules when the Ford pulled up to the curb and stopped.

Lovell House looked just as it always had, tall, cold, and stony gray. A little more worn and shabby, perhaps, and no longer quite so much like the evil castle in the book of fairy tales. But even so, standing there on the wide driveway, Gib was definitely feeling faint stirrings of the terror-stricken little boy in the square collar. Suddenly he sensed that Mr. Thornton was watching him. When their eyes met, Mr. Thornton turned back to the motorcar and pulled a saddle out of the backseat.

"Here," he said, "take this with you." And when Gib hung back, staring at him in astonishment, he added, "Take it. According to Miss Hooper, Mrs. Thornton gave it to you some time ago."

So Gib walked back across the marble entry hall and into the headmistress's office carrying a duffel bag and the beautiful roping saddle that had belonged to Julia Merrill of the Rocking M Ranch. The saddle that his own mother, Maggie Whittaker, had once ridden on. And even though he felt sure he wouldn't be allowed to keep it, for the moment it seemed to make a great difference. Somehow just the heft and the good horsey smell of it steadied his thoughts and firmed the beat of his heart.

Like the house itself, Miss Offenbacher still looked stern and forbidding and, at the same time, a little more worn and shabby. But her nutcracker jaw was just as firm, and the braids that coiled around her head still looked like fat gray snakes. And if Gib was surprised and distressed to find himself back in her office, she certainly seemed to be just as amazed and displeased to find him there. She was beginning to say so when Mr. Thornton pulled out a checkbook and began to write.

The two of them talked then in low voices for a long time. At one point Miss Offenbacher shook her head and said some things about "against the rules" and "highly irregular." But when Mr. Thornton picked up his checkbook and started to put it back in his pocket, she nodded hurriedly and said something that started with the word *however*. And then the check writing began again.

In the end Gib was told to report to Senior Hall, where, for the time being, he was assigned to bed number five. And then, just as he had feared, Miss Offenbacher said, "But he can't be allowed to keep that saddle, of course."

Another long discussion followed. Watching and listening, Gib could catch only occasional words and phrases. Right at first he heard the word *saddle* quite a lot, but after a while it began to seem that the whole drift of the argument had changed to who was going to have the last word. At one point Gib almost grinned; it was going to be hard for either one of those two to back off, seeing as how neither one of them had ever had much practice in coming in second. But at last there was another picking up of the checkbook, which seemed to turn things around a bit, and it began to look like Mr. Thornton might come out ahead at the finish line.

Before he left, Mr. Thornton said, "My wife and I want to stay in touch. Mrs. Thornton will be wanting to hear from the boy on a regular basis. And if all is well there will be . . ."

Mr. Thornton's voice dropped then, and there was another long discussion, but at last the check stayed on the desk and Gib was dismissed and told that he should not come down to supper that evening, but starting the next morning he would be expected to follow the regular schedule, which he no doubt remembered. "Breakfast at six o'clock, seniors report to Mr. Harding's classroom by six-thirty, and again at twelve-thirty for afternoon chore assignments."

A few minutes later Gib Whittaker walked into Senior Hall carrying a duffel bag and a saddle, and ran into Jacob and Bobby and three new boys as they were washing up for dinner.

CHAPTER
34

When the senior boys began to come back into the dormitory that night, Gib was still lying on his bed, not asleep really, but deep in a backward-drifting dream like the ones that always seemed to send Hy off into long-ago times and places. So when he heard a voice, Jacob's voice, saying, "All right, Gib, tell all. Give us the lowdown," it took a minute for him to get back to the present. The present, and Senior Hall in the Lovell House Home for Orphaned and Abandoned Boys.

Pushing himself to a sitting position, he shook his head to clear it, stared at Jacob's familiar but strangely altered face—a wider face, with harder, more watchful eyes—and said, "Okay, okay. What shall I . . . What do you want to know first?"

"Well, how about what got into Offenbacher? How come she let you back in?"

So Gib started to tell all of them—there were others

who had arrived by then—about the checkbook, and then stopped to ask, "But what did Miss Offenbacher say at supper? Why did she say she let me back in?"

Jacob shrugged. "Not much that made any sense. A bunch of stuff about how you had returned due to 'unforeseen circumstances' that were very unusual, and that the rest of us had better not think that we'd be allowed to come back if we ever failed an adoption."

Gib couldn't help smiling. "Unforeseen circumstances, huh?" he asked, and when everybody nodded he asked them all to keep it under their hats, but that the "unforeseen circumstance" was a check written on the Longford Consolidated Bank and signed by Henry J. Thornton himself. They all grinned knowingly and Jacob said, "Word is that the money old Mrs. Lovell left has just about run out, and the place is going to have to shut down if they don't find some more somewhere." And a minute later he added, "Oh yeah, and she also told us that we weren't to talk about it. And especially, we were absolutely forbidden to ask you about it."

Then Bobby asked what it had been like. "Was it real bad, Gibby?" he wanted to know. "Did you get starved and froze and everything?" Bobby hadn't changed much. He still gave you the feeling that he'd be real disappointed to hear that things don't always turn out as bad as you expect them to.

"No, not starved," Gib said, and then to prove the point he got out what was left of Mrs. Perry's sandwiches and passed them around. That took a while. Everyone had to open them up and admire the thick slabs of real ham and then watch carefully to be sure no one took a bigger bite than the next guy.

It wasn't until the sandwiches were just a mouthwatering memory that Gib got started telling about the Rocking M. He started in about Hy but hadn't gotten very far before his throat began to tighten and he couldn't go on. He had to swallow hard twice before he could say, "Look, guys. I'm dead tired right now. I'll tell you the rest tomorrow. Okay?" It was just about silence time anyway, so they reluctantly agreed, and Gib was allowed to get into bed and close his eyes.

But it was then that the bad part started. The part about really facing up to the fact that he wasn't going to see Hy or any of the others again. To his surprise, to not ever see Livy again was one of the most painful thoughts, even though there had certainly been times when he'd figured that he'd seen just about as much of Olivia Thornton as he could take.

For quite a while he didn't dare even let himself think about Black Silk. To think about walking into her stall and hearing her soft welcoming nicker. To let himself remember the wild excitement of letting her go full out, soaring over the rough ground as if . . .

The lump in his throat warned him then that he had better stop it or he was, for sure, going to do something embarrassing. Someday, he promised himself, he would be able to think about her again without it hurting so much. Someday, maybe, when years had gone by and he was an old man. But in the meantime he would put his mind on things about the Rocking M that didn't hurt as much, like the crabby old milk cow, and the chickens, and Bobby, the cocky little field mouse. But that started him worrying about how Bobby was going to manage now that he'd come to depend on . . . And suddenly he was crying. Crying so hard that he had to stuff his fist in his mouth and cover his head with the pillow so that no one would hear.

The next day everything was back to normal. To the kind of day that had been normal for Gibson Whittaker before the third of May in 1908. There was the breakfast of lumpy oatmeal; four hours in the classroom, in Mr. Harding's classroom trying to listen carefully and keep your eyes wide open for trouble; midday dinner; chores; supper and, soon afterward, silence. It wasn't easy, and according to Jacob, it was going to get worse, at least for Gib.

"Harding's got it in for you worse than ever," Jacob said. "I been watching him and I can tell. He's just biding his time, but he'll find something to get you for before long. And Offenbacher too. I'm guessing that they took Thornton's money to let you stay because they needed it so much. Offenbacher pretty much had to let you bust one of her favorite rules, but they don't have to like it. Mark my words, Gibby, you better watch your step or they're going to find a way to take it out on your hide."

But days passed and nothing very bad happened, at least no Repentance Room assignments for Gib, nor any painful sessions with Mr. Paddle. Still, Gib couldn't help feeling that Jacob was right when he said that Mr. Harding and Miss Offenbacher were just biding their time and that nothing had really changed.

Miss Mooney hadn't changed much either. She was still as warm and welcoming as ever, and still as overworked. Gib could tell she was curious about how his time with the Thorntons had been, but she was way too busy taking care of almost thirty juniors to spend much time talking about it. Too busy to talk and too unwilling to say anything much about the situation at Lovell House.

And just as it had always been, the nights were the worst. Days were packed full of work and people, but after the silence bell rang there was always lots of lonely time to think and dream, just as he'd done when he was a little kid. But it wasn't as easy now to conjure up a comforting hope dream because his mind insisted on picturing only one family and one house. And while a hope dream needs to be a soft, hazy possibility, for Gib the Rocking M was far too sharp and clear, and no longer any kind of possibility.

But there was still the saddle. When nothing else

worked and the night dragged on and on, he would pull the saddle out from under his bed and put it across his chest. Somehow the touch and smell of the worn, horse-scented leather made the future seem more like something that might be worth waiting for.

CHAPTER

35

Jacob went on insisting that Offenbacher and Harding were just biding their time, but a month went by without any real changes. It was almost October before Jacob's prediction seemed to be coming true when one day, after he'd dismissed the class, Mr. Harding said, "Take your seat, Gibson. I need to talk to you."

Jacob looked back from the doorway, his face showing a lot of sympathy and more than a little bit of "I told you so." And Gib's heart missed a few beats as he returned to his desk. But it turned out to be a false alarm. All Mr. Harding wanted was for Gib to write a letter to the Thorntons saying how great everything was at Lovell House.

"Holy moley," Jacob said later when Gib told him and Bobby about it. "Did he tell you every word to write?"

Gib shrugged. "Mighty near. Leastways he had me write it first on a slate and let him check it out before he let me put it on paper." He grinned. "Said he just wanted to check my grammar. But he made me leave out a part where I said I surely did wish they'd write to me."

"Well, anyway," Bobby said, "you got to write a letter to somebody. How come the rest of us don't get to write no letters?"

Jacob snorted. "Because the rest of us don't know any people who can write big checks to the orphanage. Right, Gib?"

Gib guessed that Jacob was right about that. It looked like he could write the Thorntons anytime he wanted to, if he said the right things. But if any of them, like Mrs. Thornton or Miss Hooper—or anyone else—ever wrote to him, he probably would never get to see it.

It wasn't until almost a month later, on a bitterly cold November day, that it suddenly became clear that Jacob also was right about Mr. Harding just biding his time. It started in the classroom during a geography test, when Gib dropped his pen and Harding accused him of doing it on purpose so he could lean forward and get a look at Albert's test. It wasn't true, of course, but there was no use arguing, and that afternoon Gib got reacquainted with Mr. Paddle.

There were four other rule breakers in the room that day, and afterward they all said that Gib got harder swats and more of them than anyone else. And sure enough, it was the very next day that Miss Offenbacher sent for Gib and, the minute he walked into her office, she told him to go get the saddle.

236

"My saddle?" Gib asked.

"Yes, bring it here to the office," Miss Offenbacher said, and returned her attention to the papers on her desk.

Gib was on his way to Senior Hall, wondering what had made Miss Offenbacher change her mind about letting him keep the saddle under his bed and wondering where he would have to keep it now, when he saw Buster on his way down to the laundry room with a big basket of dirty linen. Buster seemed glad of an excuse to put the basket down for a minute and rest his back, and when Gib said he wanted to ask him something Buster immediately guessed what it was about.

" 'Bout that there saddle?" he asked.

Surprised, Gib said, "Yes. How'd you know?"

"Because Offenbacher told me I'd be taking it with me when I go to the feed store. Said I was to sell it to Mr. Kelly."

"Sell it?" Gib felt like a fist had slammed into his middle. "But she said I could keep it. Why'd she change her mind?"

Buster shook his head. "Didn't say. All she told me was that I should pick it up in the office and take it to Kelly's Feed and Tack." He looked hard at Gib and his sharp-boned face twisted with the kind of disgusted anger that Gib remembered from before. Anger mostly at himself when he was about to take a stupid risk by talking too much. Or for worrying about some little kid when he had plenty of worries his own self. "She didn't

237

tell me anything more, but I heard her and Harding talking about something that was in the paper."

"In the newspaper?" Gib was astonished. What could something in the newspaper have to do with Miss Offenbacher's changing her mind about the saddle?

Buster was watching Gib closely. "Seems like maybe they ain't going to get some money they were counting on." Leaning over to pick up his basket, he looked up at Gib through narrowed eyes and added, "Mighta had to do with somebody dying?"

It sounded like a question. Like maybe Buster thought Gib would know what he was talking about. Gib shook his head slowly, making his face say that none of it made any sense to him.

Buster's shrug looked even more depressed and disgusted than usual. After he headed down the stairs Gib went on up to Senior Hall and sat down on his bed. It was almost time for class to begin, and no one else was in the room. He pulled the saddle out from under the bed and sat for a while with it on his lap. Then he put it over his shoulder and went out into the hall. He stood for a moment looking down toward the main staircase before he turned himself around and headed in the other direction.

Up on the fourth floor in the deserted servants' wing were some secret places he'd discovered back when he and Jacob used to get in a quick game of hide-and-seek between chore time and supper, and he remembered one place that was pretty hard to find. He left the saddle there at the back of a tiny closet. Then he went all the way back down to the ground floor and knocked on the door of Miss Offenbacher's office.

She was sitting at her desk when he came in, and she looked up sharp and hard as always, but wondering too. Wondering what he was doing there without the saddle.

"Gibson?" she asked, so he told her straight out. "Ma'am, I just can't do it. I can't bring my saddle down here and give it away." He was talking fast, sure she was going to interrupt him and start yelling, but for a minute she didn't. Just sat there, she did, looking downright astonished, like she couldn't believe what she was hearing.

When you came right down to it, Gib couldn't either. Couldn't believe he was standing there in front of Miss Offenbacher trying to tell her why he couldn't give up the saddle when he didn't rightly know himself. But he did try. "It used to be Mrs. Thornton's special saddle that she learned to ride on, ma'am, and my own mother rode on it once. And she said it was mine now. Mrs. Thornton did, that is, and I just feel like . . ."

But Miss Offenbacher had stopped listening. Getting to her feet, she stomped toward Gib so that he flinched and turned his face away. But she went right on past him and out the door, and when she came back Mr. Harding was with her.

That day Mr. Harding beat on Gib until his arm wore out. Not five or ten whacks, as usual, but just on and on, only stopping now and then to ask if Gib was ready to do as he was told. Then he would start up again until finally his face was all red and he was breathing so hard he had to sit down to catch his breath. And then, after his breathing had quieted some, he marched Gib up to the Repentance Room.

As he shoved Gib through the door he said, in between puffs and gasps, that he'd see him again tomorrow and the day after that and the day after. . . . Then the door slammed and his voice faded away, mingling with the sound of his retreating footsteps. Gib sank down to the floor, coiled himself up into a ball, and buried his face in his arms.

CHAPTER

36

It was cold in the Repentance Room. Gib's back and legs ached from the beating and the rest of him ached from the cold. As suppertime came and went and the hours crawled by, Gib thought mostly about what he had done—and why. It wasn't like anything he'd ever done before. Always before he'd pretty much gone along with whatever seemed necessary. Not because he was afraid, but mostly because it didn't seem to matter all that much one way or the other. But this was different. He didn't know why, but this was really different.

It wasn't until sometime in the middle of the night that he gave up on trying to understand why he'd done what he did and began to think some more about why Miss Offenbacher had changed her mind about letting him keep the saddle. Buster had said something about her not getting some money she was expecting. Everyone knew that the orphanage was short of money, but it didn't seem likely that what they could get for one old saddle was going to make that much difference.

But that got him to thinking about the other things Buster had said, and it wasn't until then that he came up with a strange and shocking idea about what might have happened.

Buster had said that Offenbacher wasn't going to get the money she was expecting because somebody had died. So what if that somebody was Mr. Thornton? Mr. Thornton, who had like enough promised Miss Offenbacher more checks if Gib kept writing letters saying he was doing just fine.

Right at first Gib couldn't believe it could be true, but the more he thought about it, the more likely it seemed. Other memories came up. Memories of how Mr. Thornton had come home sick so often last summer, and of how bad he'd looked that day in the Model T when he stopped to take his medicine.

It was a strange and worrisome thing to think about there in the lonely darkness of the Repentance Room. There he had been, Mr. Thornton, the banker, Mrs. Thornton's husband, Livy's father, and Hy's boss, a part of everybody's life at the Rocking M. Gib could bring him to mind as clear as day, reading his papers at the kitchen table, driving Caesar and Comet or the Model T to work every day. And now he was gone forever.

After a while Gib tried to make himself feel better by remembering all the hard, mean things about Mr.

Thornton. How he had not wanted to adopt Gib and had not even wanted him as a farm-out until he had to, because of Hy's broken leg. And how he managed not to see things or animals or people he didn't like. But Gib's mind kept slipping around to how Mr. Thornton had let him keep his saddle, even though he'd had to pay Miss Offenbacher something extra to get her to say yes.

But that brought up why Gib was where he was at the moment—back in the Repentance Room. It looked like Miss Offenbacher must have decided that now that Mr. Thornton was dead, nobody else had enough interest, or maybe enough money, to do anything to help Gibson Whittaker. It was a bitter thing to think about, but it did seem to be the sorry truth.

By the time a sleepy-eyed, grumpy Buster came to let him out, Gib had decided that whatever happened, he could not give up. Now more than ever he couldn't let them take away his saddle. Jacob, who had waited up for Gib as usual with a chunk of dried-out bread, was shocked when Gib told him. "You can't mean that, Gibby," Jacob said. "They'll beat the life out of you. You'd have been better off to have just up and run away."

"Maybe so," Gib said. "I thought about it. Yesterday when I went up to get the saddle, I really did think about just walking out of here. But with winter coming on and . . ." He stopped and they both sighed, and Gib knew they were both thinking about Georgie.

"But what you're doing won't do any good," Jacob said.

"They can find your old saddle if they really set out to do it. They must know it's here in the building. You didn't have time to take it anywhere else."

Gib nodded. "I know," he said, "but what matters is that I can't just give it up to them. I can't just hand it over, like it was their right to have it and decide what happens to it. It's like—it would be like I might as well give up on living."

So Jacob threw up his hands and said he *gave up* on trying to save Gib's neck, and stomped off to bed. And sure enough, the next morning they had hardly finished eating breakfast when the monitor came in with a notice for Gib to report to Miss Offenbacher's office immediately.

Gib went down the stairs to the grand entrance hall of Lovell House slowly, keeping his mind on what his feet were doing so he wouldn't be able to think too far ahead. Just one foot in front of the other, until he came to the office door, knocked, went in—and saw that there were two people in the room.

Another person, a woman, was seated across the desk from Miss Offenbacher. Her back was to Gib and she was wearing a wide-brimmed hat, but her voice was strangely familiar. And even before Gib's eyes told him who it was, he suddenly felt himself grinning.

"Good," the woman was saying. "I'm glad we're beginning to understand each other."

Miss Offenbacher's flushed and scowling face didn't

look all that understanding. "I won't—you can't—I did not say that I would allow—"

"Oh, but I'm sure you will," Miss Hooper interrupted, "when you consider what Mrs. Thornton's continued patronage can do for Lovell House." She turned then and said, "Run and get your things, Gibson. I'll be waiting out front in the buggy."

A few minutes later Gib walked back down the grand marble staircase and out through the wintry air to where Miss Hooper and Hy were waiting in the buggy. Hy in the driver's seat and, back in the buggy, Miss Hooper, wrapped in a heavy cloak and lap robe. Gib was putting his saddle on the backseat when Miss Hooper handed him a package and an envelope. There was a heavy mackinaw in the package and Gib put it on before he climbed up to sit with Hy.

"Storm coming?" he asked, looking at Hy's bad leg, and Hy rubbed his knee and grinned and said how it surely was beginning to feel that way.

Gib opened the envelope then and took out a bookmark. Another narrow piece of heavy cardboard with a picture painted on it, much like the one Livy had given him for his birthday. Only this time the picture wasn't just of a black horse's head. Instead it was a really well-done painting of the whole horse—and of a rider who was sitting on its back. The rider hadn't turned out quite as well. The arms were too long and seemed to bend in the wrong places and the face was a kind of lopsided circle. Could have been a picture of most anybody, except for the long brownish yellow curls that corkscrewed out from the lopsided head in every direction.

Down at the bottom in little tiny writing it said, "We missed you." Gib was still looking at the bookmark when Caesar and Comet trotted smartly into a sharp turn and picked up the pace as they headed toward home.

AFTERWORD

William Solon Keatley 1878–1955

Gibson Whittaker's history is not the same as that of my father, but many of the events in Gib's story were inspired by tales my father told of his early life in a Nebraska orphanage and as a farm-out on neighboring ranches. Required to do a man's work when he was eight years old, beaten, mistreated, and, yes, sent out into a blizzard without his mittens, causing his hands to be so severely frostbitten that they very nearly had to be amputated, he survived to become a kind-hearted, patient man with an unquenchable sense of humor and an uncanny ability to communicate with horses.

But while he spoke only sparingly and with an amazing lack of bitterness about his terrible childhood, my father would talk endlessly about his life as a wrangler whose job it was to green-break wild mustangs fresh from the open range. Roundups, stampedes, rustlers, and rattlesnakes played minor roles in a continuing epic whose major theme was horses he had known and loved. I grew up loving his stories, his horses, and him, and Gib Rides Home is my tribute to his memory.

Zilpha Keatley Snyder

Be sure not to miss the newest novel
by Zilpha Keatley Snyder.

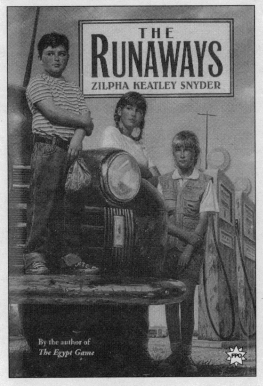

0-385-32599-1

On sale now from
Delacorte Press.

chapter

14

Dani didn't believe one word of it. She didn't believe that Mr. and Mrs. Smithson were planning to put a bunch of body parts together into one and zap it with a whole lot of electricity and make it come to life. Right after Pixie left she told Stormy so. "And that stuff about the body parts proves it," she told him. "Like she just didn't have time to figure out that chapter of the story yet."

But Stormy only shook his head solemnly. "She knows that chapter," he said. "She already told me about it. They're going to get them from the graveyard. She already told me they were getting some from the Rattler Springs graveyard."

Dani almost fell over laughing. "That's ridiculous. That

graveyard is just an old boomtown burying place. I don't think anybody's been buried there for years and years. Not since the silver mines gave out."

"Yeah?"

"Yeah. All you have to do is read what it says on the grave markers. They're all, like, around 1900, or even before that."

"Well, what's wrong with that?" Stormy asked.

Dani was still grinning. "Well, what's wrong with that is . . . ," she said in her most sarcastic tone of voice, "what's wrong with that is, the Rattler Springs graveyard's too old. In the Frankenstein story he went to the graveyard right after someone died. Right away after, so there would be a real body, with skin and muscles and stuff like that. What kind of a monster are the Smithsons going to make out of some practically ancient bare-boned skeletons?" She was grinning when she asked, but she could tell immediately by the look on Stormy's face that he didn't see anything very funny about the idea. And after she'd had a moment to think it over, she didn't either. Nothing particularly funny about the idea of a bare-boned skeleton who'd been zapped to life, stalking around the desert looking for . . . Just like Pixie said, it was the kind of thing you didn't want to talk about. Or even think about.

She was still trying not to think about it when Linda came back from the movie and Stormy finally took himself off home. And later that night when Linda was sound asleep on the daybed couch, Dani, in her stifling hot bedroom, had something else to not think about besides Gila monster truck drivers. Rolling over for the umpteenth time, she shook her head hard to chase away a cloudy procession of monsters in greasy denims, only to have them replaced by a parade of living skeletons.

The next morning she was still thinking about what Stormy had said about the graveyard. Thinking about how ridiculous the whole thing was. She grinned, wondering what Pixie would say when she heard how old the graveyard was. But just wait, Dani told herself. When she finds out that story won't work, she'll think up a new one.

It turned out that she'd guessed right about that one. About Pixie having a better answer the next time she showed up. The only part she didn't guess was how soon that was going to be. Like early afternoon on the very next day.

When Dani opened the front door Pixie came right in without waiting to be invited. "My dad had to come in to make a phone call, so I came too," she said. "I can stay until he comes back."

"Comes back?" Dani asked.

"Yes, comes back to town. At five. Like always."

Dani looked over at the alarm clock on the daybed end table. It was just a little after two o'clock. "Well," she had just started to say when Pixie came on in and started taking some books out of a big handbag made of woven straw. "I brought some more of my books," she said. When she finished with the books she looked around and asked, "Where's Linda? I thought you said she was going to be off today."

Dani shrugged. "Yeah, I guess I did. The bookstore is

closed but she took an extra job today. She's baby-sitting for the Grahams while they're in Las Vegas."

"Oh." Pixie looked around uneasily, even glancing out the window as if she were hoping her father might still be out there so she could change her mind and go home. "Oh, I thought . . ."

She didn't finish telling what she'd been thinking, but Dani could guess. Pixie had probably figured that if Linda were home Dani wouldn't have a chance to ask any hard-to-answer questions about the Frankenstein thing. Like where you could get body parts in the desert, for instance. Maybe she hadn't come up with any good answers yet. And maybe she never would, because there just weren't any good answers. Dani was beginning to enjoy herself, watching Miss Supercool Pixie squirm a little.

"And Stormy?" Pixie asked.

Dani shook her head, trying not to look smug. "Not here," she said. "Gone somewhere on an errand for his mom's boyfriend. One of her boyfriends, anyway."

Another good try, Dani thought. Without Stormy, Miss Storyteller Smithson had lost her best audience. Sitting down in Linda's rocking chair, Dani said, "About that question I was asking when your folks showed up last night. You know, the one about where they were going to get parts for their monster? I was just wondering if you could talk about it today. And I was also wondering if you knew that the Rattler Springs graveyard hasn't been used for about fifty years. So don't bother to tell me about the graveyard."

Pixie nodded slowly. Climbing up on the daybed, she arranged herself carefully, smoothing her skirt down over her knees and crossing her feet in their scuffless saddle shoes. At last, when she was all ready, she sighed and said, "I shouldn't have told Stormy that story about the graveyard. I just did it because—because . . ." She stopped and sighed. The sigh was slow and solemn but when she glanced up Dani got a glimpse of her eyes and there was nothing slow or solemn there. "I didn't tell him the truth because it was just too— too . . ." She shuddered before she went on. "The truth is, well, my folks have this great big electric freezer. And back where they used to live there were lots of graveyards. So . . ."

Dani got the picture. And even though she certainly wasn't trying to see it, there it was, flashing before her eyes. A picture of what you might have seen in Frankenstein's freezer chest if there'd been such a thing in those days. Something cold and dead and coated with icicles and fuzzy frost. In spite of herself, a shudder crawled up her back.

"That is the most gruesome thing I ever heard of."

Pixie nodded enthusiastically. "I know." Then she sighed and her thumbnail-movie-book face flipped from eager to excited and then to sad-eyed pitiful. "And that's not the worst of it. That's not anywhere near the worst of it."

"Oh yeah?" Dani said.

"Yes. There's another part that's a lot more terrible." Pixie's voice was still gloom and doom but the quick upward flick of her eyes was something else.

"Okay. You might as well tell me." Dani sighed, trying to

make her face and tone of voice say that she certainly wasn't promising to believe it, but she wasn't going to let Pixie get away with stopping at that point. "I mean, you can't say there's a worse part and just stop there."

This time Pixie's sigh was particularly long and mournful. "No, I guess you're right." Squaring her shoulders and lifting her chin, like a person getting ready to face up to something terrible, she began, "Well, see, the other day the generator stopped for just a few minutes but then, after they got it running again I heard them talking. They didn't know I was listening but I was. And what I heard them say was . . . Well, my father said that it would have spoiled"—she paused—"er, everything if the electricity had been off much longer. And then . . ." She paused again, and when she went on her voice was like the music in a movie when it tells you something terrible is about to happen. "And then, I heard my mother say that they could still go on with the experiment if they could use parts from one other body."

Dani tried not to gulp before she asked, "Another body? Who—Whose body?"

Pixie nodded. "She didn't say. At least not exactly. But she nodded—toward my room."

Dani's gulp turned into a gasp. "Toward your room?" she repeated, sounding like a stupid parrot.

"I told you it was too terrible to talk about," Pixie said. She was looking down, hiding her eyes again. She didn't look up as she said, "But that's why I have to go with you, when you and Stormy run away."

15

That did it. It was the very next day that Pixie started being included in the running-away plans. At least more or less. Not that Dani really believed her crazy story, because she didn't. Or at least most of the time she didn't. It was only in the middle of the night, when it was easy to believe all kinds of impossible things, that she wasn't entirely sure.

Dani had gone to bed that night telling herself scornfully that Pixie sure had a big imagination. But it happened to be a dark moonless night and a black desert wind was snaking around Rattler Springs, rattling shingles and sifting sand in around doors and windows. Lying there listening to the whispering wind and crawling sand, Dani drifted off into a dream about trying to climb into a truck and being grabbed by someone who looked a lot like a Frankenstein monster except he seemed to be wearing saddle shoes and a pleated blue skirt. She woke up then and stayed awake for a long time, thinking and worrying.

The next morning, when she told Stormy about Pixie's latest tall tale, he didn't doubt any of it. Not for minute. They were in the kitchen at the time. Linda had just left for work and Stormy was at the table fixing himself a huge bowl of cornflakes. Dani had hardly finished the telling when Stormy stopped pouring milk on his cornflakes, smacked his fist down on the table and said, "Yeah. I thought so."

"You thought what?" Dani asked.

"I thought they might be going to do that."

It was a ridiculous idea. Dani tried to tell Stormy so. Tried to tell him that it just wasn't possible that parents, even slightly weird ones like the Smithsons, would ever think of chopping up their only kid. Not even if they happened to be mad scientists who needed some body parts for a Frankenstein-type experiment. "It's just too crazy," she told him. "And besides, parts from an extra-small ten-year-old just wouldn't work. Not unless they were planning to make a midget-sized monster."

But nothing she said seemed to make any difference. There just wasn't any use trying to convince Stormy that everything Pixie said wasn't the truth, the whole truth and nothing but the truth. She was still trying when Stormy interrupted by saying, "So, how soon can we leave?"

"Leave?"

"How soon can we run away? Can we do it today?"

Dani stared in amazement. "You know we can't leave yet. Not until we get some more money for tickets."

"But—But how about stowing away in a truck, like you said before?"

"What?" Dani was amazed and indignant. "I told you I changed my mind about that," she practically shouted. "So just forget about it. Okay?" She glared for a moment before she added, "Oh, I get it. So now we're suddenly in a big hurry, are we? When I was the only one who needed to get away fast, you kept slowing things down, and now suddenly we're in a big rush."

Stormy did his thoughtful eye-rolling thing for so long that Dani was getting ready to punch him before he said, "But *you* weren't about to get chopped up."

At that point Dani got up, stomped out of the house and slammed the door. She was still sitting on the back steps and Stormy was still in the kitchen eating cornflakes when a car door slammed out on Silver Avenue. Dani jumped up, dashed through the kitchen and beat Stormy to the front door. It was Pixie, of course.

Pixie came into the house on tiptoe, her fiery blue eyes darting wildly. Tiptoeing up to Dani, she whispered, "Can we talk? Is your mother gone?"

Dani backed away. "Yeah, she's gone," she said in a normal, nonwhispering voice, not wanting Pixie to think she was going along with whatever game it was she was playing now. "What's up?"

Still whispering, Pixie said, "That's what I was going to ask you. What are we going to do today? You know"—her voice got even lower—"about running away." She looked at Stormy. "Stormy told me how you were looking for a truck to stow away in."

"He what?" Dani said.

Stormy was shaking his head but Pixie didn't seem to notice. "Didn't you, Stormy?"

"No, I didn't. Not anymore I didn't." He gave Dani his guilty, squinty-eyed look. "We changed our minds about that. Now we're going to go on the bus."

Pixie looked a little disappointed. "Oh," she said, sighing. "I thought the stowaway idea sounded exciting." She sighed again, but after she glanced from Stormy to Dani and back again, she began to nod. "Oh. Okay," she said. "On the bus." Going over to the daybed, she climbed up and smoothed herself down the way she always did when she wanted to take time out. She was wearing safari-type khaki shorts and a blouse today, the kind with lots of extra straps and pockets. When she got all arranged she said to Dani, "Tell me about the bus. What's it like on a bus?"

"What's it like?" For a moment Dani thought she must be kidding, before she realized that poor little rich girl Pixie, who rode around in fancy custom-built cars, probably didn't know much about bus riding. "What's it like to ride on a bus?" she asked in a sarcastic tone of voice. "Well, for one thing you have to pay before you get on. So that's kind of the problem right now. We don't have enough money for tickets."

"Oh?" Pixie was definitely interested. "So what are we going to—?"

"We did a lemonade stand," Stormy interrupted eagerly. "We made three dollars and ninety-eight cents. But we had to stop because of Ronnie."

"Ronnie? Ronnie Grabler from school?" Pixie asked, and that really got Stormy started. He was jumping around like he always did when he told a story, but when Dani tried to stop him Pixie said, "No. Let him tell me. I want to hear about it."

So Dani went into the kitchen, dumped what was left of Stormy's cornflakes in the garbage and sat down at the table to wait until Stormy's "Gus the Hero" story was finished. But while she was waiting she began to get a new idea. The idea had to do with how adding a rich kid to their plans might actually be helpful. She was still fooling around with some new possibilities when Stormy and Pixie came into the kitchen.

Pixie was still laughing about Ronnie and the grease pit, but she stopped when Dani asked her how much money she had.

"Money? How much do I have?" Pixie asked. Fishing around in the pockets of her khaki shorts she brought out some change and started to count it. "Thirty-four, thirty-five," she said. "I have thirty-five cents."

Dani sighed. "No. I didn't mean in your pockets. I mean, don't you have some saved up at home, like in a bank or something?"

Pixie shook her head.

"How about an allowance? You have an allowance, don't you?"

Pixie thought for a moment before she shook her head again.

"You don't?" Dani made it clear she found that hard to believe.

Pixie looked thoughtful. "I did once," she said. "But they kept forgetting to give it to me and I kept forgetting to ask for it, unless I wanted something. So now I just ask when I want something, and they give it to me."

Stormy was looking excited. "Could you ask for enough for the tick—" he'd started to say when he saw that Dani was laughing. "Stop that!" he yelled. "I didn't mean tell them it was for tickets. I meant she could say—she could just say . . ."

Dani decided to come to his rescue. "Okay, okay," she said. "I know what you meant." Then she said to Pixie, "I think he means could you ask them for the money for something else, something kind of expensive, like a bicycle maybe, and then take the money and buy tickets instead?"

Pixie nodded thoughtfully. "Umm, maybe," she said. "Maybe. I could try it anyway. How much does a bicycle cost?"

Stormy was all excited. "I know. I know," he started yelling. "Wait. I'll get it. I'll go get it." He dashed away, out the back door and down the steps. *Slam, clomp, clomp, clomp, slam* and a bunch more *clomps*. For a kid who could be so quiet when he tried, it was amazing how noisy he could be when he wasn't trying.

"Where's he going?" Pixie asked. "What's he going to get?"

Dani led the way into the living room. "Who knows. Something about a bicycle, I guess."

It was a good guess. In about three minutes the slamming and clomping started all over again and Stormy burst into the room, carrying what looked like a magazine but turned out to be a bicycle catalog. A ragged, worn-out catalog full of pictures of beautiful, expensive bikes. Climbing up on the daybed beside Pixie, Stormy opened it to an illustration of a really fancy Schwinn bicycle. Someone, Stormy no doubt, had underlined and circled that particular bicycle in red and black crayon and had drawn yellow shooting stars all around it.

"See. That's it," he said. "That's a Black Phantom. It's my favorite. My favorite for a long time." He sighed, a long sad sound. "Costs too much." He pointed to where, under the picture, it said $175.00.

"A hundred and seventy-five dollars. Holy moly!" Dani said. "I didn't know a bicycle could cost that much. Linda didn't pay that much for our truck." She and Pixie looked at the picture and then at each other and then at Stormy. He was staring at the bicycle with the same kind of glassy eyes he got when he listened to a story.

Dani took the catalog away from him and slammed it down on the coffee table. "So," she said to Pixie, "I suppose if you asked your folks for a hundred and seventy-five dollars to buy

a bicycle they'd say, 'Sure thing. How soon do you want it?' "
She laughed, expecting Pixie to laugh too. But she didn't.

Instead she nodded solemnly. "They might," she said. "My mother used to ride bicycles and she wanted me to learn how, but mostly I live with my grandmother and where she lives there isn't any flat place to ride so I never did learn."

"You mean you don't even know how to ride a bicycle?"

Pixie nodded. "Only a little. I tried a few times on a friend's."

"And you think they might give you that kind of money to get you something you don't even know how to ride?"

Pixie tilted her head thoughtfully. "Maybe. I think so. I didn't know anything about chemistry when they bought me a very expensive chemistry set. My dad said I would learn by doing. But my grandmother took it away from me when I set the basement on fire."

Dani sighed and changed the subject to some other money-raising ideas she'd been thinking about, halfway reasonable ones like baby-sitting or dog walking.

So that was more or less the end of the bicycle conversation, and as far as Dani was concerned the end of even thinking about it. But when the Smithson tank pulled up in front of Dani's house that afternoon and Pixie ran out to meet it, she must have taken Stormy's bicycle catalog with her. At least when Stormy went home he couldn't find it. He made such a big fuss about it that Dani had to read an extra chapter of *The Jungle Book* just to calm him down.

The next day was a Thursday and Pixie didn't show up all

day long. It was just about the only day she hadn't since school had been out and Stormy was really worried. He didn't exactly say so but it was obvious that he was afraid that Pixie's parents had already started collecting some body parts. Usually nothing could distract Stormy while he was listening to a story, but that afternoon he kept jumping up and running to the window every time he heard a car go by. And there wasn't any use trying to get him to think about moneymaking plans, not even for a minute.

It was fairly late in the afternoon, almost time for Linda to come home, and Dani was just about to finish a chapter when she heard the squeak of the gate hinges and then slow, unsteady footsteps on the front porch. When she opened the door there stood Pixie. Nothing else in sight. No tank-car out on the road. Just a messed-up, dirt-smeared Pixie whose face was tear-streaked—and whose hands and knees were smeared with lots of bright red blood.

"What—what happened?" Dani gasped.

Holding out her bloody hands, Pixie managed a strange, tearful smile. "I fell off my bike," she said.